the
brightest
SUNSET

The Darkest Sunrise Duet 2

ALY MARTINEZ

ROM
Martinez

Sticks and stones will break my bones, but words will never harm me.

Lies.

Words destroyed me.

"I'm sorry. She didn't make it."

"Daddy, he can't breathe!"

"There's nothing more we can do for your son."

Sticks and stones will break my bones, but words will never harm me.

More lies.

Those syllables and letters became my executioner. I told myself that, if I didn't acknowledge the pain and the fear, they would have no power over me. But, as the years passed, the hate and the anger left behind began to control me.

Two words—that was all it took to plunge my life into darkness.

"He's gone."

In the end, it was four soft, silky words that gave me hope of another sunrise.

"Hi. I'm Charlotte Mills."

The Brightest Sunset
Copyright © 2017 Aly Martinez

ISBN-13:978-1973778943
ISBN-10:1973778947

THE BRIGHTEST SUNSET is a work of fiction. All names, characters, places, and occurrences are the product of the author's imagination. Any resemblance to any persons, living or dead, events, or locations is purely coincidental.

Cover Designer: Jay Aheer
Photography: Wander Aguiar
Editing: Mickey Reed
Proofreader: Julie Deaton
Formatting: Stacey Blake

the brightest SUNSET

The Darkest Sunrise Duet 2

PROLOGUE

Porter

"CATHERINE, WAIT," I CALLED, TUCKING MY WALLET INTO the back pocket of my navy slacks. I glanced down to Hannah, who was cooing in her infant car seat and enjoying the ride as I carefully jogged out of the cardiologist's office.

"Buckle up, Travis!" Catherine snapped, her voice high and agitated.

"Why can't I ride with Dad?" he whined, slamming his door.

Turning sideways, I shuffled between the parked cars, reaching them as she put it in gear. Quickly, I patted the hood of her car before she had the chance to back out.

She jumped, and her chocolate-brown gaze swung to me.

Lifting Hannah in the air, I clipped at the windshield, "Forgetting someone?"

Her eyes flashed wide, and her mouth formed the word,

"Shit." After putting the car back into park, she swung her door open and climbed out. "I thought you had her."

"I *did* have her. But I have to go back to work."

She stomped over and took the baby carrier from my hand before going back to the car, snatching her car door open, and loading her inside.

"Dad! Can I ride home with you?" Travis yelled through the open door.

I bent low so I could see him. "Sorry, bud. I have to get back to work."

His face fell and a pang of guilt hit my stomach.

"How about, when I get home, we play some video games?" I offered as a substitution.

His face lit. "Okay!"

Our conversation was cut off when Catherine suddenly slammed the door. She reached for the handle on the driver's side, but I caught her arm.

"Are you going to be pissed all day?"

She angled her head back to look at me, attitude etched on her face. "Yeah, Porter. It's safe to assume I'm going to be pissed all day."

I groaned. "Christ, Catherine. He doesn't agree with your plan. I'm thinking we should listen to him. After all, he is the doctor."

Her glare turned murderous. "And he's my son!"

No one wanted to hear that their child needed a heart transplant, but we'd known that day was coming. Travis was four when I'd entered the picture and he'd already been di-agnosed. Catherine had told me then that, with the right medications and treatments, he'd get better. But one trip through Dr. Google and I had known she was wrong. Dilated Cardiomyopathy wasn't something that could be cured. Treated? Yes. Managed? Yes. Fixed? Only with a transplant.

But, for four years, she'd convinced herself otherwise. She'd spent countless hours scouring the internet, looking for information on Travis's condition. She binged on success stories and failures of children with a similar condition to the point of obsession. Just that morning, she'd presented the cardiologist a proposed treatment plan, complete with drug names and dosages that she believed would cure our son. It had not gone over well when I hadn't backed her up.

"You have no idea how much it's going to hurt to lose him. I'm going to die right along with him. I can't…" She trailed off when her chin began to quiver, and she nervously glanced over her shoulder to where Travis was sitting in the back seat.

"Hey," I breathed, wrapping her in a hug. "It's going to be okay."

"Is it?" she croaked.

"Yeah. It is," I lied.

"I don't think so." Her shoulders shook as she broke down in my arms.

It was rare for Catherine to show that side of her emotions. But, then again, she hadn't been sleeping well since Hannah was born. While my baby girl was healthy as a horse and slept like a dream, Catherine woke up numerous times a night to check on her. I'd spent a small fortune on at least a dozen different monitors and booties that supposedly triggered an alarm if the child stopped breathing, but nothing could quell Catherine's fears.

I hadn't thought much of it in the beginning, but the older

Hannah got, the worse Catherine got too. Any time I woke up in the middle of the night, Catherine was always awake, staring into the baby's bassinet, her hand resting on her chest as if she were waiting for it to stop moving. She'd smile and play it off, saying that she liked to watch her sleep, but I knew it was more. Though, any time I tried to talk to her about it, she'd brush me off and make an excuse to change the subject.

"What if he dies before they find a donor?" she whispered into my neck.

My arm tensed around her. "Catherine, honey. He doesn't even need the transplant yet. We still have options."

Her breath shuddered. "I can't lose him again, Porter."

"Nobody is losing him," I whispered adamantly. "I swear on my life Travis isn't going anywhere. Let's listen to the doctors and try to be optimistic before we worry about a transplant."

"You don't understand," she cried. "If anything happens to him—"

I leaned away to catch her gaze. "*Nothing* is going to happen to him. You have to stop acting like the transplant is a death sentence. It could save his life."

"It could also *kill* him. And then where would that leave me?"

Her. That was where all of these conversations went. How would his death affect *her*? Forget about the rest of us. Hell, forget about Travis actually losing his life.

It was always about Catherine.

Frustrated, I blew a ragged breath out and released her. "We're all going to be fine." Looking over her shoulder, I found Travis's dark gaze aimed at us, so I shot him a placating smile and added a wink to sell it. Then I whispered to Catherine,

"You need to get it together. He's watching us. We can't expect him to be strong if we're breaking down."

"Oh, God forbid he learn that his mother is imperfect."

Grinding my teeth, I bit out, "That is not what I meant. No one is saying you have to be perfect."

"I need to go," she snipped, snatching the car door open.

Fuck. Now, she was pissed again *and* upset.

I didn't dare say anything else as she climbed inside. I'd already set her off; there was no point exacerbating it.

Digging my keys out of my pocket, I walked to my car, the heavy weight of guilt settling over me. I hated that she was hurting, but it was virtually impossible to deal with her when she got like that.

Our relationship had changed so drastically over the years. I told myself that it was to be expected in marriage. Especially when you threw in the stresses of a sick child, an unplanned pregnancy, and then the exhaustion of having a new baby.

But, if I was being honest with myself, we'd been falling apart even before that.

I loved my wife, but it wasn't like it used to be. Love was now a conscious decision rather than a feeling.

I climbed into my car with a sick sense of dread rumbling in my stomach.

I needed to go back to work, but my conscience wouldn't allow it.

My family needed me.

My *wife* needed me.

So, when her car turned left out of the parking lot, mine did too.

Traffic was light, and it didn't take more than ten minutes

to get to our exit.

"Hey, Karen. It's Porter. I'm not going to be back today," I told my secretary as I followed Catherine off the highway.

"Oh no," she said softly. "Doctor's appointment didn't go so well?"

"Not really, and I think it's best if I take the rest of the day…"

The words died in my mouth as I watched in horror as Catherine's car drifted to the shoulder. My skin tingled as I waited for her to correct it, figuring she'd only looked down for a moment or maybe turned to hand something to the baby.

But not even her brake lights flashed before she hit that guardrail. The sound of metal hitting metal was piercing, but knowing my family was inside that car made it deafening. My stomach clenched as I lost sight of them over the side of that bridge.

It all happened so fast I almost didn't think it was real. I slammed on my brakes, my phone flying out of my hand as I came skidding to a halt.

Darting out of my car, I raced toward the cement railing. I'd driven over that bridge every day for over two years, but in that moment, I couldn't remember what was beneath it. All I could imagine was my family careening into oncoming traffic or a bed of rock below. As messed up as it was, a blast of relief tore through me when I saw her car sinking. Water seemed like the best-case scenario.

Catherine could swim.

So could Travis.

But Hannah….

I took off at a dead sprint, racing down the rocky

embankment. I slipped about halfway down and slid the rest of the way on my ass, but I didn't let it slow me.

"Catherine!" I bellowed as I dove into the frigid water, fully clothed.

Adrenaline had taken over.

It took no less than seven hundred years for me to reach that car. And with every second that passed, when none of their heads popped up from beneath the surface, a part of me died. I was vaguely aware of people yelling from the bridge above me, and then I caught sight of a man diving in from the opposite side of the banks. But I was too focused on my never-ending journey to reach my family to find any relief in the fact that people had stopped to help.

By the time I got to the car, the front end was underwater, the roof only partially visible and the bumper stuck up in the air like a buoy.

My heart was beating so fast I feared it would explode. And that would have been fine by me, as long as it lasted long enough for me to pull them to safety first.

"Travis!" I frantically tried to pull open his door to no avail. "I'm coming, buddy. Hang tight!" I yelled, clueless if he could hear me or not. But I needed him to know I was there. I slammed my fists against the window, but the only thing that broke was the flesh on my knuckles.

My mind swirled to figure a way in until I heard his garbled cry.

"Dad!"

My heart stopped, and the world shattered around me.

"I'm right here! I'm gonna get you out!" Cupping my hands on either side of my face to block the sun out, I peered inside the back window.

Catherine was holding him, his back to her chest, a trail of blood pouring from her eyebrow. Travis's head was craned back, his hands flailing against the surface, and his mouth hung open, gasping for air as the water rose around them.

"Catherine!" I screamed, beating on the glass. "Unlock the door. Give him to me!"

But she didn't move. Her cold, glassy eyes stared back at me as her chin disappeared under the water.

"No! No! No!" I chanted. Scanning the inside of the car, I noticed the front windows had been opened an inch and water was pouring in through them.

After sucking in a lung full of air, I went under water. The river was murky and I could only make out shapes rather than details, but I managed to find the front door. Hooking my fingers over the top of the glass, I pulled as hard as I possibly could, using my feet to add leverage. It shattered in my hands, the bite of the glass not even registering amongst the adrenaline.

After climbing into the sinking car, I headed straight up to the air pocket.

"Get out of here!" I yelled at Catherine, shoving her and Travis toward the window.

Panic ricocheted through my system when I saw Hannah's car seat completely submerged. Frantic, I went straight to her and began the tedious task of getting her out with shaking fingers. Each strap and buckle becoming a victory all of its own.

When I got back to the pocket, I pushed Hannah into the air. She wasn't conscious, but I prayed that air would miraculously fill her lungs. My stomach dropped when Catherine was still there, Travis kicking and flailing in her arms, his face almost completely under water.

"Come on!" I ordered, grabbing the front of her shirt and pulling her with me as I swam out as fast as I could with my unmoving daughter tucked in the crook of my arm.

When I breached the surface, I lifted Hannah's tiny body high, treading water while I spun in a circle, waiting to see the tops of Catherine's and Travis's heads emerge.

For those seconds, everything stopped.

Nothing around me mattered.

Not the freezing water.

Not the sirens blaring in the distance.

Not the bile clawing up the back of my throat.

Nothing but those two dark heads I so desperately needed to pop up.

"Come on, come on, come on," I prayed as I swam to the bank with what I feared was my baby girl's lifeless body.

I didn't even look at the person I handed her off to before I started swimming back toward that car, my heart in my throat, the weight of a thousand ships on my chest.

Only the bumper was sticking out of the water, and it felt as though my life were slipping away with that car.

Where the fuck were they?

Diving back down, I swam back into the car.

And then, all at once, every single question I never wanted answered became clear when I once again found them inside that car.

I couldn't make out much, but I saw her arms wrapped around his shoulders, his arms floating at his sides. I grabbed him first, shoving hard off the seat of the car, but he was suddenly snatched from my grip. My lungs were on fire, but getting them out wasn't an option. I was going to die in that car before I gave up on them.

And as I struggled against her hold on him, I feared that was exactly what was going to happen.

There was no more air pocket, just a sinking car trying to take my wife and son to a watery grave.

It took a second for me to realize what was happening. At first, I thought she had to have been disoriented, maybe injured from the wreck.

But, with every passing second, the truth became unmistakable.

Her hands clawing at mine.

Her feet kicking me in the stomach.

Her hold on him fierce and visceral.

It wasn't an accident; every move she made was strategic to keep him with her—and to keep them both in that car. The final straw was when I felt the seat belt wrapped around the two of them anchoring them in place. She hadn't been in that seat belt the first time I'd pulled them out. There was no possible way that could be mistaken as anything except a deliberate and calculated move.

I froze. The day I met her at the local farmers market flashed on the backs of my eyelids. I'd gone to buy tomatoes and come home with a family.

My vision tunneled, darkness surrounding me, my body screaming for oxygen. But what had once been an attempt to save them both became a brawl of epic proportions.

My hands were no longer shaking, and my fears morphed into anger. I cursed and screamed that I hated her, nothing but a few bubbles carrying the message. But I didn't stop until I was able to pry my son from her arms.

I didn't look back as I headed for oxygen, leaving her there to die.

Only she wasn't alone. Porter Reese, the man who'd vowed to love her in sickness and health, the man who'd held her when she'd cried and smiled at her when she'd laughed, the man who had promised her forever, died in that river beside her.

And it took three dark, twisted, and hate-filled years before he was ever found.

ONE

Charlotte

I COULDN'T BREATHE.

I couldn't talk.

I couldn't even formulate a rational thought.

Pure instinct took over.

The blood in my veins caught fire as I spun out of Porter's arms. Lucas—my son, Lucas—screamed as I took him with me. The inherent need to flee overwhelmed me.

Porter was faster though. One of his hands caught me above the elbow, his grip straddling the line between rough and firm. "Charlotte, stop!" he growled. "Don't do this. He is *not* Lucas."

I heard his *words*, but they felt like hollow syllables filled with weeks of deceit.

Tom appeared beside me, his voice low and sinister. "Let her go, Reese."

"Give me back my son," he snarled, his fingers biting into

1

my bicep.

Defiantly, I held his stare. "He's *my* son."

"Dad!" Lucas cried, struggling against me. But there wasn't a force in the world that could have taken him from me.

Not this time.

Not again.

Not *ever* again.

Porter snaked an arm down and took his son's outstretched hand, holding it as he closed the circuit between the three of us. "It's okay, bud. This is just a big misunderstanding." His gaze lifted back to mine, his eyes hard. He looked nothing like the man I'd been falling in love with.

Probably because that man didn't exist. This was the real Porter. The one who'd kept my son from me for the last ten years.

"Back up!" I demanded, my legs shoulder-width apart, my arm latched around Lucas's chest, my whole body roaring and ready for war.

"He's *not* Lucas," he declared through clenched teeth.

"Back—" I started to repeat my demand, but my voice lodged in my throat.

His face softened, and so did his hand as the fraud that I'd always thought was my Porter appeared. "Let him go and we'll figure this out. Everything's going to be okay."

It was crazy, but my heart squeezed in response to his familiar words, even as my head screamed for me to hate him. "Why would you do this to me?"

"Why would I do this to *you*?" he asked, his face taking on the strangest mixture of disbelief and astonishment. "Charlotte, I have no fucking idea what is going on right now.

2

All I know is that you have your hands on my kid and you're calling him the name of your dead son. Sweetheart, there isn't much in this world I wouldn't do for you. But I draw the line when it comes to my children."

We stared at each other.

The ultimate showdown.

Mother versus Father.

Nature versus Nurture.

Heart versus Soul.

Neither of us willing to back down.

Not when it came to holding on to the only sunlight we were ever going to get.

"I'm giving you one more chance, Reese. Let her go," Tom growled behind me.

Porter's gaze locked on mine. "When she lets go of Travis, I'll let go of her."

Travis.

His son.

Fuck that. This was *my* son.

The sound of his name lit a fuse inside me. Years of pent-up anguish suddenly detonated, feeding a white-hot rage I'd never felt before.

It was visceral and ugly.

But it came from the most beautiful place in my heart.

The place that had been created and filled the day my little boy had been born.

The place I couldn't forget no matter how hard I had tried over the last ten years.

The place that harbored the most agonizing pain a person could experience, unleashing it like a vile animal sent to destroy me every single morning I woke up without him.

The place that was currently whole for the first time in *ten fucking years*.

My face vibrated as I screamed at the top of my lungs. "His name is Lucas!"

In my explosion, my grip must have slipped, because suddenly, my son broke free of my arms. He went straight to Porter, who protectively stepped in front of him.

"No!" I yelled, diving forward. Porter's hand came up and landed in the center of my chest, where he held me back.

And then all hell broke out around us.

Tom caught me around the waist, dragging me back as Charlie went after Porter.

"Get inside, Travis," Porter grunted as his face was roughly shoved against the brick beside the door.

My little boy stood there frozen, horror contorting his pale face as he peered up at Porter. The woman at the door moved fast in his direction. She grabbed his shoulder and curled him into her front, hiding his face as she backed him inside the house.

"Lucas!" I screamed, kicking and clawing my way out of Tom's hold.

"He's not Lucas!" Porter shot back while Charlie clicked the cuffs around his wrists.

But he was.

And I'd just lost him all over again.

"No. No. No!" I cried when the door shut behind him. "Lucas!"

"Charlotte, look at me," Porter called while Charlie read him his rights. "It's not him. I swear to God it's not him."

"Shut up, Reese," Tom growled, tucking me tight against his front.

Porter's body flexed and strained as he fought to get to me. "Charlotte, please look at me, sweetheart," he begged in such a sweet voice that I swear I could feel the actual shards of my heart breaking in my chest.

Not even ten minutes earlier, I would have happily gotten lost in the sea of his blue eyes for all of eternity.

But that was before I'd had something to fight for.

"Lucas," I choked out, tears flowing down my chin.

Tom brought me into a bear hug with my arms pinned at my sides, but my fingers still stretched as though they could reach the door.

"Please," I begged softly. "Please give him back to me."

"Charlotte!" Porter continued to bellow, but I kept my eyes trained on the wooden door that separated my heaven from my hell.

My son was in there.

My baby.

And he was alive.

My knees suddenly buckled and the fight left me on a ragged sob. "Oh God. That's really him."

Tom held me tight. "We need to get to the station."

"How…how is this possible?" I stammered.

"I have no fucking idea, but I need you to get it together. The sooner we figure it out, the sooner you can get him back."

My whole body was trembling, but with those words, my heart slowed and my lungs inflated.

I was going to get him back.

He was going to come home.

He was going to be mine again.

I hadn't been brave enough to dream about that moment in a lot of years.

And there it was—a reality.

And, for some fucked-up reason, I couldn't comprehend why my chest still hurt.

Turning, I got my answer.

Porter was in the back of the patrol car, his arms secured behind him, his wide eyes locked on me, fear carved into his face, and his mouth moving in the pattern of my name.

And that was when I realized we'd only thought we knew the darkness.

"Charlotte!" Brady called as he came barreling through the door to the conference room, his wife, Stephanie, hot on his heels.

I'd been waiting, and thus pacing, for over two hours. My body was numb, and my brain was scrambled. Nothing felt real anymore. Over the course of the day, I'd woken up next to Porter—the man I was falling in love with—found out my son was dead, grieved my son on the side of a bridge, found out my son *wasn't* dead, and then seen him for the first time in nearly a decade. And all of this had happened just before discovering that the man I'd woken up next to had known where my son had been all along.

Yeah, there was nothing that could have prepared me for a day like that. I was living it and still couldn't wrap my head around it.

It felt like a nightmare in the middle of the sweetest dream.

My heart was breaking while simultaneously being filled to the cusp.

"Hey," I whispered, crossing my arms over my chest to ward off the chill that usually accompanied Brady.

He stopped a few feet away, grabbed the back of his neck, and cut his eyes to the floor. "Tom says you saw him."

I swallowed hard and did my best to keep my voice from shaking. "I did."

He lifted his gaze, a million contradictory emotions dancing within. His usual death glare was nowhere in sight as he asked, "What's he look like?"

My heart melted. Brady was a dick, but his son was alive too, so I put our history aside for a minute and answered him.

"You. Me. Everyone." I paused, my chin quivering. "No one."

His lean body was on mine in a second. I couldn't remember the last time I'd touched him. We both loved our son, but Lucas was the product of a one-night stand. Brady and I hadn't been lovers in any regard. Friends? Maybe once. But not in a long time.

The hug was awkward at best. No one could deny that Brady was an attractive man, and he'd aged well over the years. But the hug was all wrong.

His arms were tight, but he wasn't warm like Porter.

Jesus, why was I still thinking about Porter?

Oh right, because I'd have given anything for him to be standing in that room with me. His body protectively embracing me. His lips at my ear as he told me that it was going to be okay. His darkness stilling the world for me. Him having had nothing to do with my son's disappearance.

In other words, pipe dreams for the insane.

I shouldn't have needed him the way I did. That was my first mistake with Porter: depending on him when reality got too hard. But I had. And, at the moment, if my life had ever fit into a category, "too hard" was exactly it.

My mind still couldn't make heads or tails of why he'd had Lucas. The obvious being that he'd taken him. The not so obvious? Hell, I still didn't have a theory on that one.

Hooking my arms under Brady's, I returned his hug.

"I…uh…" Stephanie stammered. "How about I wait in the hall and give you two a minute alone."

Brady released me and leaned toward his wife, brushing her blond curls away before gently cupping the curve of her jaw. He whispered something soft in her ear that caused her lids to flutter shut. When he was done talking, she tipped her head slightly, offering her husband her mouth.

He pecked her once. And then again before breathing, "I love you."

It was so sweet and unlike anything I knew of Brady, so much so that it momentarily made me uncomfortable.

He watched her with warm eyes as she glided to the door, and then, with one last glance over her shoulder, she was gone.

Brady turned back to me and blew out a ragged breath.

He stared at me.

And I stared at him.

Neither of us uttered a word, but it was as far from my comfortable silence with Porter as one could get.

Finally, in a shaky voice, he said, "It's over. It's really over."

But it didn't feel like it was over to me. I was terrified that it was just getting started.

And I had no one who could understand that feeling. I was getting everything I wanted and it still scared the shit out of me.

And, for reasons that could only be explained by the staggering loneliness caused by Porter's sudden departure from my life, I chanced a darkness confessional with Brady.

"I'm scared."

His eyebrows drew together. "What? Why?"

Questions.

I focused over his shoulder at the door. "I have no idea."

"That's crazy, Charlotte. This is what we've been praying for since day one. And it's finally happening. Don't be scared."

Judgment.

Steeling myself and ignoring the pain in my chest, I flashed a tight smile at him. "You're right."

Faking it.

He inched closer and lowered his voice, but it wasn't the soft one he'd used with his wife. It was as if he were whispering over gravel. "You have to get that shit out of your head. I don't want him seeing that. He needs to feel like this is a good thing. Because it *is* a good thing. Lucas is coming home."

I swallowed hard. "Right. I'm sorry. I'll get it together."

Apologies.

Noise at the door drew my attention. Mom came walking in, two cups of coffee in her hands.

"Hey, Brady," she said, suspiciously glancing between the two of us.

She'd been with me since I'd arrived, only stepping out of the room twice. Once to check with Tom to see what was going on. And the other about ten minutes earlier to get coffee—and

I suspected once again to check in with Tom, seeing as he was following her in.

He came straight to me. "Brady tell you?"

"I hadn't had a chance," he replied, moving away.

Alarm pricked the hairs on the back of my neck. "Tell me what?"

Tom's face softened as he whispered, "It's him."

"I know," I replied.

I could have told him that back at the house. I had not one single doubt about it. I don't know how I had known, but the minute I'd seen him with fresh eyes, I had known he was mine. Yet Tom's next words still hit me harder than I ever could have imagined.

"No, Charlotte. It's *really* him. Remember the prints we lifted off his toys when he was first taken? They're a match. He's yours."

Proof. Undeniable. Absolute. Final.

I blinked again, but this time, panic blasted through my system, causing my vision to go blurry.

"Oh, honey," my mom breathed, sidling up beside me before pulling me into her side.

"So, when do we get to see him?" Brady asked, ignoring my impending meltdown.

"Well," Tom started. "He's down the hall. So I guess that's up to you. I passed off all the paperwork to Brady's attorney, who's running them out to Judge Gratham's house now. Assuming he's got everything he needs, he said he'd sign off on a temporary custody order until a formal hearing can be set. Social Services is going to want to have a word with you two before you can take him home, but you can meet him any time you'd like."

"Temporary custody?" Brady snarled.

"It's a formality," Tom assured.

In a quiet voice, I found the courage to ask, "What about Porter?"

Tom's face got hard. "What about him?"

"Yeah," Brady snapped. Taking a giant step in my direction, he parroted Tom but with a lot more attitude. "What about him?"

I licked my dry lips and flashed my gaze between the two men. "I mean...what's going on with him? How is he involved?"

"He kidnapped our son!"

Tom lifted his hand to silence Brady. His face remained hard, but his voice gentled. "Our guys are still working with him, trying to figure out his role in all of this." He pointedly cut his gaze to Brady for a second before sweeping it back to mine. "It *doesn't* appear that he was part of the actual abduction. Lucas was already four when he met Catherine Reese. We believe her child died, though we don't have a cause of death yet. It appears to be of natural causes. Maybe SIDS or some underlying medical condition. Who knows? She was probably distraught, saw Lucas at the park, and took him to replace her son. Just slipped him right into Travis's life."

I lifted a shaky hand to cover my mouth and breathed, "So, Porter didn't know?"

"You have got to be fucking kidding me here," Brady seethed.

Tom turned a scowl to Brady, who was all but vibrating beside me. However, with my old friend hope infusing my system, I didn't give a damn.

"Answer me," I demanded.

"We don't know," Tom replied. "I refuse to believe he didn't figure it out before he started pursuing you. The fact that he was dating the biological mother of the child his wife kidnapped doesn't sit well with anyone here. Way too much coincidence there for it not to be suspicious. But we're going to get to the bottom of it. Trust me on this, babe. You do *not* have to worry about Porter Reese anymore."

Oh, but for the way my heart felt like it had been put through a strainer, I did.

Brady fisted a hand on his hip, his other pinching the bridge of his nose, and spat, "I can't believe you were dating that piece of shit."

My throat got thick and a cold chill sent a shiver down my spine, but I gathered enough attitude to choke out, "I don't particularly care what you believe and don't believe, Brady."

My hands were shaking, so Tom caught the back of my neck and pulled me into his chest, his words aimed at Brady. "Think of it this way. It all worked out. We found him, okay? Let's worry about Lucas now."

Nodding, I sucked in a deep breath, hoping that it would somehow ease the turmoil and panic inside me.

It didn't.

But I could pretend better than anyone on the planet.

And, as the hours wore on, I had to do just that.

TWO

Porter

SAT ON THE WRONG SIDE OF THE TWO-WAY MIRROR IN THE police station, my arms folded on a small table, my face buried between them.

My chest empty.

My mind jumbled.

My stomach in knots.

My entire fucking life unrecognizable.

I'd only thought the day Catherine had driven off that bridge was the ultimate betrayal.

Boy, had I been wrong about that.

"Answer the question, Porter."

"No!" I snarled, lifting my head to stare into the eyes of the third cop who had come in to ask me the same fucking question over the last two hours. "I don't know what you're talking about."

"So, Catherine—"

"No!" I snapped, shoving off the table and rising from my chair.

My nerves were shot.

The fingerprints were a match. DNA was still being processed, but I'd given up holding out any hope that that wasn't going to match too.

Travis was Charlotte's son.

And nobody in the entire fucking Atlanta police department would believe that I didn't have something to do with it.

"Catherine didn't tell me shit. Okay? I didn't even know her when Lucas was kidnapped. Travis was four years old when we started dating, four and a half when we got married, five when I adopted him, and eight when she killed herself. And, during those years, never, not once, did she ever mention that she stole a baby off a fucking playground."

He stared up at me, his face unreadable, and slowly flipped a file folder open. "Okay. Now that you mention it, let's talk about the day your wife died."

My chin jerked to the side as though he'd struck me. "What?"

He kicked my chair, shoving it toward me, and tipped his chin for me to sit down. "It says here that you were on the scene the day of the accident. You were the first person in the water and the last one out. You managed to get both of your kids out, but somehow, your wife was still inside that car when her body was recovered?" He rocked back, folded his hands in front of him, and watched me expectantly.

Ice chilled my veins. "Yeah. That's what fucking happened," I bit out. Leaning forward ominously, I stabbed my finger at the file he was reading from. "Does it also say how I nearly drown in that car, trying to save her? How she fought me with her dying breath? What about that it was no *accident* at all? She purposely drove off that bridge. So let's get one thing straight. My wife didn't die—she killed herself."

His face remained impassive. "The two of you have an argument that day? Things get a little heated? She had some bruising on her body when it came in."

I barked a humorless laugh. "Are you shitting me here?"

"Not at all, Mr. Reese," he drawled in a thick Southern accent.

"She drove off a fucking bridge!" I exploded, my voice echoing off the walls. "With my children in the car. We were all bruised and battered that day. That was not limited to Catherine. Travis was—"

"Lucas," he corrected.

I glared at him with wide and wild eyes, daring him to correct me again.

He lifted his hands in feigned surrender, a cocky smile playing at his lips. "Just wanted to make sure we were on the same page." He tipped his chin to the chair again. "Sit down, Porter."

My jaw ticked as I held his gaze. "I did everything I could that day. And I will *not* stand here and listen to you insinuate otherwise. My wife kidnapped a kid, a fucking baby, and you're going to sit here and pretend that she wasn't crazy enough to kill herself. Pull your head out of your ass, put down the torches, and look at the facts. I was *not* part of any of this. My only crime here is falling in love with a little boy who belonged to someone else."

"Sit down, Porter."

15

I sucked a breath in through clenched teeth, desperately trying to find a calm that I feared no longer existed, and begrudgingly sank down, fury fizzling in my chest.

Propping himself on his elbows, he steepled his fingers and tapped them against his lips. "The boy is going home with his mother."

I choked on my own breath as a freight train hit my gut.

Intertwining my fingers, I rested my hands on my head, frantically trying to fill my lungs with oxygen.

"The boy is going home with his mother."

Oh God. This was not happening. They were going to take him from me.

"No. No. Listen," I started, but I had to stop to clear my throat when it became impossible to speak around the boulder lodged inside. "He's sick. He needs a lot of medical—" I couldn't finish, because if the pain ricocheting inside me was any indication, I was literally dying.

He spoke as if the Earth hadn't fallen out of orbit. "Then it's probably a good thing his mother is a doctor."

I found no relief at the mention of Charlotte. My chest actually ached more.

"Oh God," I groaned.

"We've been questioning the kid, Porter. And I swear, if one fucking detail of his life doesn't match the statements you've given us, I'm going bury you under the jail. Murder, kidnapping, child endangerment, the whole nine."

"You can threaten me with whatever the hell you want, and it's not going to change the truth." My mouth dried and I couldn't keep the overwhelming emotion out of my words as I croaked, "I haven't done anything wrong, but you're taking my son away from me. Bury me under the jail now, because I'm not coming back from this."

I dropped my head into my hands, my mind swirling with the cold, hard truth of my new reality.

His chair scraped against the floor as he stood, but I didn't bother to look up.

"We'll let you know if we get any hits on your daughter," he said.

I shot to my feet, my metal chair flipping over behind me with a bang. "You're checking my daughter?" I shouted, incredulous. "For fuck's sake, I was there the day she was born!"

His face remained stoic and empty as he pulled the door open. "Then we shouldn't have any problems."

The door swung shut with a loud click.

How was this happening?

I'd woken up that morning with a family and a woman I was falling in love with.

And, now, my life was in shambles.

"This can't be real," I whispered, allowing my head to fall back between my shoulders. "Wake up. Please, God, just let me wake up," I pleaded with the universe.

How the hell did they expect me to let him go? Shit. What would I even tell him? *Sorry, Travis. Your mom stole you, and now, you have to go live with strangers?*

"Oh God," I choked out.

Would I even get to see him again to explain what was going on? The knife in my stomach twisted.

And then there was Hannah. She loved her big brother more than anything. How would I ever explain this to her?

Hell, I could barely breathe knowing this. Telling her

17

should push me right off the edge.

"Fuck!" The scream tore from the core of my soul—or at least what was left of it. I picked my chair up and slammed it to the floor as hard as I could.

The crack was loud and jarring, but it did nothing to make me feel better. But then again, after this, I wasn't sure there was a better anymore.

Welcome to your new life, Porter Reese.

"Goddamn it, Catherine. I hate you so fucking much!" I roared at the heavens.

Or, in this case, hell.

THREE

Charlotte

"**B**REATHE," MY MOM WHISPERED, HOLDING MY HAND tight as I stared at the tall, wooden door.

Brady on my left.

Tom at my back.

My little boy just a few feet away.

We were waiting for the social worker to give us the go-ahead to enter.

"I'm fine," I lied.

"You're crying," she said softly, giving my hand a squeeze.

I swiped my fingers under my eyes, nervously flashing my gaze to Brady to make sure he hadn't seen. Luckily, he was staring down, enthralled with his shoes.

"Are you going to be okay in there alone with Brady?" she whispered.

I looked at my mom. She was crying too. The only difference being that hers were tears of joy. She hadn't stopped smiling since Tom had shown her a picture of Lucas he'd snapped on his phone.

I grinned tightly. "Lucas is in there, Mom. Brady won't even know I'm there."

She brushed the hair off my neck. "Okay. Well, if he gives you any shit, you let me know." She lowered her voice and leaned in close. "I have no problem kicking his ass."

My lips tipped up into something that I thought resembled a smile. "Thanks, Mom."

She winked. "Any time, baby."

We all jumped when the door suddenly cracked open. A young woman with thick, red curls piled on the top of her head appeared, wearing a navy blazer and a warm smile. "Ms. Mills? Mr. Boyd? You can come in now."

My whole body tensed as if I'd been invited to take a stroll down death row, but Brady moved fast, all but plowing me over as he raced inside.

"Lucas?" he called.

I had no choice but to follow him. That's what good parents did. They ran to their children, relief flooding their systems, tears overwhelming them.

They didn't stand frozen with fear in the middle of the hallway, nerves rolling in their stomachs while contemplating the merits of throwing up.

No. That's not at all what good parents did.

Which probably explained why that was exactly what I did.

"Go," my mom urged, giving my shoulder a gentle shove.

Stiffly, I shuffled into the room with my heart in my throat, prepared to face the little boy I'd failed so many years ago.

"Stop!" Lucas yelled before I'd fully cleared the door.

Brady was squatting low, his shoulders shaking with quiet sobs. Lucas was tight in his arms, his face the picture of horror, as he frantically tried to shimmy his way out of Brady's embrace.

"Mr. Boyd," the social worker scolded.

We'd been briefed for twenty minutes on how to handle this reunion. During this time, we'd learned that our son had specifically asked that we not touch him. I assumed that this request had been given after my showdown with Porter back at the house. He'd also asked that we called him Travis. The social worker had urged us to stay calm and keep our emotions in check. And further that, if we found ourselves unable to keep it together, given the emotional altitude of that day, we were simply to excuse ourselves so as not to upset him.

And there Brady was, not ten seconds after he'd entered the room, breaking every last rule.

"Brady!" I hissed.

"I'm sorry," he said, reluctantly letting him go and rising to his feet. "I…" He trailed off and used the back of his arm to wipe his face. "Shit. I'm so sorry. I thought I could do it." He looked over his shoulder, his red, tear-filled eyes slicing through me as he said, "It's Lucas."

"My name's Travis," he said, scrambling away, not stopping until his back was against the wall. His lungs wheezed as he added, "Travis *Reese*. And I want my dad."

I slapped a hand over my mouth. After the last ten years, I didn't have much of a heart left, but what was left shattered into a million pieces.

"I am your—"

"Brady, don't!" I snapped, cutting him off.

He wanted his dad.

And, suddenly, so did I.

Squaring my shoulders, I took a step toward my son. "Hey, Travis. I'm Charlotte."

His dark-brown eyes, which matched my own, slid to me, and then he sank deeper into the corner.

"I won't touch you. I promise," I assured, moving to the other side of the large conference table. I slid a chair out and sat. "I'm really sorry about all of this. Especially for when I freaked out on you back at your house. That won't happen again. You have my word."

He didn't move or relax, but he continued to wheeze.

I had no idea what I was doing in the parenting department, but his every strangled breath was my territory.

"I met you once before today. At the doctor's office. You stood outside with my best friend, Rita, while your dad and I talked. Do you remember that?"

He nodded cautiously, and just that little acknowledgment sent a wave of relief crashing over me.

"Okay, good. Then maybe you remember that I'm a doctor too, right?"

He nodded again.

"Perfect," I breathed, leaning forward on my elbows. "Now, listen. I know you're scared. Today has been crazy. But I really need you to sit down and try to relax. Did you bring your inhaler?"

His eyes cut to the social worker in question.

"Oh, right," she said, jumping into action. After grabbing a small, neon-green backpack from the corner, she carried it straight to me. "There's a lot of medicine in there. I'll be honest. I have no idea what's what."

I smiled up at her. "I think I can manage."

And then my smile fell when I unzipped the bag. She hadn't been lying. There was *a lot* of medication inside. At least thirty prescription bottles, a full nebulizer including extra mouth pieces and tubing, packets of individual saline, and three inhalers.

Jesus, my baby was *sick*.

Clearing my throat, I laid the inhalers on the table and then zipped the bag back up, saving that nightmare for another day.

I recognized all of the labels, but handing him the right one wasn't going to win me any affections.

"Hey, Travis?" I called. "Do you remember which one of these Dr. Laughlin gave you for emergencies?" I hazarded a glance up and found that he'd come unstuck from the corner.

"The blue one."

Another one of those waves of relief hit me.

I purposely picked up the wrong one. "This one?"

Shaking his head, he took a step toward me and lifted his finger to point. "No. That one."

I offered it his way. "Right. Of course. Silly me."

He stared at me for several seconds, the scales in his head visually shifting as he weighed his options. Then he lifted his gaze to Brady, who was still standing near the door.

Understanding dawned on me.

"Brady, can you do me a favor?" I asked while keeping my eyes on Lucas. "Go see if you can find a first aid kit for me."

"What? Why?" Brady asked.

I peered over my shoulder and flared my eyes at him. "Please. Now."

His back shot straight for only a second before he rushed from the room.

"Why do you need the first aid kit?" Lucas asked.

"Oh, I don't. He was just making me nervous standing back there." I winked.

And then it happened. The most beautiful thing I had seen since the day he was born.

He grinned.

It was small. Almost imperceptible.

But it was there. And it was aimed at me.

Do not cry. Do not cry. Do not cry.

I bit my tongue to distract myself and shook the inhaler. "Here."

His frail body swayed as he walked toward me. I tried not to stare, but I was desperate to memorize his every movement. To fill even the deepest recesses of my mind with ten years' worth of memories, for fear that that moment was all I would ever get.

Our fingers brushed as he took the inhaler from my hand, and I once again ignored my overwhelming urge to cry.

Sucking in hard, he drew the medicine into his lungs with a practiced ease. He immediately started coughing, so I pushed the chair beside me out for him to sit. He didn't delay in accepting the offer.

"There ya go," I soothed, my fingers twitching to touch him. But I somehow managed to keep them in my lap.

His brown eyes flicked up to mine, but he didn't say anything.

"Better?" I asked with a tight smile.

He nodded and then asked, "When can I see my dad?"

My stomach clenched, but I answered him honestly, "I don't know."

His chin quivered, and his eyes filled with tears. "I want to go home."

Oh God.

There was nothing I wouldn't do to ease that pain for him. Even if that meant igniting my own.

Digging in my back pocket, I retrieved my cell phone. Then I pulled up my text messages from Porter.

The last message had been a picture he'd taken of us the night before. I was laughing, my eyes closed and my mouth wide. He was kissing my cheek, his nose smooshed against my face, and despite that his lips were puckered, he was still smiling. We'd been lying in bed when he'd told me that we needed a picture together. I'd argued because, well…it was what I did with Porter. So he'd held me down, tickled me, and then snapped the selfie when I'd been too lost in hysterics to stop him. When I'd sobered, he'd shown it to me, and it was the craziest thing. I hadn't recognized myself. That woman was beautiful. And not in the conventional way where her hair and makeup were done to perfection, but rather because the woman in that picture looked genuinely happy.

And the man kissing her did too.

The truth was that, while I couldn't think about my relationship with Porter without acknowledging the darkness, I also couldn't think about us without remembering the overwhelming, life-altering happiness I felt when we were together.

I'd never forget his proud grin as I'd used his phone to

message the picture to myself.

My whole body ached as I briefly looked at that woman on the screen. She'd only been gone for a matter of hours and I already missed her. I wasn't brave enough to look at Porter. I was barely keeping my emotions in check as it was. Add his gorgeous, smiling face into the mix and I would have lost it.

Passing the phone to Lucas, I said, "This was taken last night."

He looked at it for only a second as if it were merely a picture and not the most stunning image ever snapped, which was exactly the way it felt to me.

"Are you his girlfriend?" he asked.

I shrugged. "I think I was. But today has been pretty crazy for all of us. Look, the reason I wanted to show you this is because you know your dad. He wouldn't just kiss anyone like that. He trusted me…" The L in Lucas was on the tip of my tongue, but I managed to stop it before it rolled off. "Travis." I faked a smile. "He even asked me to be your doctor when we first met. And I'd like to think that he would still trust me to do what is best for you in this situation too." A lump lodged in my throat, and my nose began to sting. I had no idea if I was lying to him or not.

I hoped I wasn't.

But I was afraid I was.

Tom and Brady were still adamant about Porter's involvement in this.

But the longer I thought about it, the more doubts I had. Though I recognized that those were probably just the hopes and dreams of the woman from the picture rather than reality.

After clearing my throat, I continued. "I know you're

scared, and I know you're overwhelmed. Because I am too. But I swear on my life I'm here for you, Travis. And despite what happened at your house today, which I will again apologize for, I think your dad would like the fact that I'm here with you too."

He blinked up at me, his thick black lashes fluttering as he struggled to beat back his emotions. "Do you know where he is?"

I shook my head. "I'm sorry. I'm just as lost as you are in all of this. I don't know what's going on outside of this room right now or what's going to happen when you and I leave, but I promise you I'm going to make it okay. Whatever that means. Whatever I have to do. I *will* make this okay." A tear rolled down my cheek, and I quickly swiped it away. "I won't let anything happen to you again. I swear."

His face softened, and his lungs still rattled far more than I would have liked, but the fear had thankfully started to fade from his eyes. "Can I text him?"

My breath flew from my lungs, and I nervously cut my gaze to the social worker in the corner.

She was watching us closely, but her expression held no answers. Not a hint of *sure, let the boy do it* or even *no fucking way*. She just stared at me like I was supposed to know how to handle this.

"Please," he whispered, drawing my gaze back to his.

Brady would have lost his mind.

But that text wasn't about him.

It wasn't about me.

It wasn't even about Porter.

It was about a scared little boy. One who, in the span of a

few hours, had had his whole life flipped upside down.

And he was *my* scared little boy, so there was not one thing, including the wrath of Brady Boyd, that could have stopped me from saying, "Sure."

His eyes lit. "Really?"

"Of course. Go ahead. I'm not sure if he has his phone right now, but he'll see it whenever he gets it back."

He smiled, big and toothy. Just like his father. And I didn't mean Brady.

Using one finger, he pecked out a message. His mouth stretched wider each time he glanced up at me.

I could have spent the rest of my life in that chair, watching him grin at that screen.

In those seconds, he looked a lot like the woman laughing in the picture, and that filled me in all the right places. I wasn't sure if that woman was gone or not, but I'd never forget the way she felt.

And, right then, I knew that my baby was feeling it too.

I heard the swoosh of the send button, and then he passed me my phone back, a bright smile still dancing on his face, slow and steady breaths flowing from his lungs.

"My sister, Hannah, would like your phone."

My inner smile fell flat, but the one on my lips remained strong. Tucking my phone back into my pocket, I asked, "Oh yeah?"

"It's purple. She loves purple."

"What color do you love?" I asked to change the subject.

"Uh." His eyes flashed around the room while he thought. "I guess green. Or maybe blue. Wait…no. Definitely green. But blue… Ugh…I don't know."

God, he was cute.

"Both are good colors."

"My dad likes blue."

My heart dipped, but I kept smiling like my mouth didn't know how to do anything else. "You're right. He does."

We stared at each other, almost like he knew he shouldn't be talking about Porter, and he was daring me to tell him to stop.

But I wouldn't. I didn't care that it felt like he was twisting a knife in my stomach. Not as long as he kept smiling at me like that.

The door opened with a creak, and I turned to see Brady coming back in, panic in his eyes, a first aid kit in his hand.

"I'm so sorry. I couldn't find one that had anything more than Band-Aids in it. One of the guys went and got this out of their car." He raked a shaky hand through his hair and asked, "What else do you need?"

"Nothing. We're all good now. Thanks for grabbing that though," I said, righting myself in my chair.

Lucas was peering up at him, his mouth in a straight line, and those nerves I'd all but erased were once again present in his ashen face.

"He's nervous, but I promise he's a good guy," I whispered to my son.

His gaze bounced to mine. "I'm hungry. Can we go get something out of the snack machine? I saw it when they brought me in."

"Uh…" I drawled. "Did it have any chocolate in it?"

"I think so."

"Then yes."

He stared at me stoically for several beats, and then that grin that healed my soul broke across his face again.

We both stood and headed to the door, but right before we passed Brady, the world disappeared.

The past.

The present.

The happiness.

The tears.

The fear.

The pain.

The longing.

The guilt.

The loneliness.

Everything was just gone.

Well, everything except Lucas as he took my hand in his.

I couldn't even pretend to control them anymore. Tears sprang from my eyes, and I turned my head so he wouldn't see them.

Emotions I hadn't felt in years bubbled to the surface. It was a miracle that I could figure out how to put one foot in front of the other.

I had missed him so damn much. And there he was, holding my hand. Of his own accord.

Doing everything I could to keep the silent sobs locked away, I allowed Lucas to lead me past Brady, who was standing with his mouth hanging open, out the door and past my mom, who was curled against Tom's side. Their eyes filled with tears as they watched us go straight to the vending machines.

Out of the darkness.

And into the light.

FOUR

Porter

IT WAS THREE IN THE MORNING WHEN MY ATTORNEY, MARK Leman, led me out of the police station.

The sky was dark, not even a star visible among the hovering clouds.

But, at the same time, the reality was so bright it was blinding.

"Porter!" my dad yelled, his long legs eating the distance between us, relief crinkling the corners of his green eyes.

Tanner was right behind him, a similar expression contorting his face.

"Where's Hannah?" I asked.

"At home with your mom," Dad answered, pulling me in for a brief hug.

The tiniest fraction of relief washed over me. At least they couldn't take her away from me. Though I had a feeling they were still going to try.

"Give me the latest?" Dad demanded.

Mark sighed. "I'm going to be frank with you, Tommy. This is just the beginning. As I told Porter, the police have nothing to hold him on, but the investigation will continue over the next few days, if not weeks. He needs to cooperate to the best of his ability."

Dad gripped the back of his neck. "Jesus Christ. Of course he will."

I didn't have much of a choice. Cooperate or lose my son forever.

And, even if I did cooperate, the latter wasn't off the table. An idea that felt like acid to my soul.

I was beyond exhausted, and my head was pounding. The intermittent surges of adrenaline my body had been feeding me all night had ravaged me.

"Where's Travis? When can we take him home?" Dad asked.

Now, wasn't that the million-dollar question?

My shoulders sagged in defeat.

Mark looked at me, but when I found myself unable to reply, he answered for me. "Temporarily, Travis has been placed in the care of his biological parents."

"No fucking way!" Tanner boomed. "He doesn't even know them."

Strangely enough, despite the fact that we'd been dating for over a month, I was starting to feel like I didn't know Charlotte, either.

I bit the inside of my cheek until I tasted blood. "Charlotte asked for an order of protection to prevent me from having any contact with Travis."

"What?" Dad and Tanner gasped in unison, their shock echoing my own.

Charlotte, more than anyone else, knew exactly what my children meant to me. I had no words to adequately explain the pain of that betrayal. It seemed to be a common thread in my life when it came to women.

"Holy hell," Tanner breathed, gripping the back of his neck.

Mark chimed in. "There will be a custody hearing next week to decide something long term. I'll be honest. We don't have much ground to work with, but we're preparing to make a case that, given his health issues, it's in Travis's best interest to remain with the only father he's ever known—at least part-time."

"Part-time?" Dad snarled.

Those two syllables feeling like a one-two knockout punch. Though, when faced with the horrifying possibility of not having him at all, part-time was the only hope I had to hold on to.

"I'm afraid so," Mark said. "And, after talking to the family's counsel, it doesn't sound like the child's parents are going to be open to this arrangement."

"Holy shit. Are you okay?" Tanner asked, reaching out to cup my shoulder.

No. I wasn't okay in any fashion. My blood was boiling, and my soul was crushed. Half of my life had been ripped away from me.

Emotion clogged my throat. "No. I'm never going to be okay with this. That's my son. And people just expect me to let him go because Catherine was a madwoman. That doesn't fucking change the fact that he's mine. He will *always* be mine."

Before I had the chance to break down completely, Tanner caught the back of my neck and stepped in front of me.

His gaze intense and his words promising. "We'll get him back."

"How?" I begged. "Please, God. Just tell me how?"

Tanner's face paled. "I don't know yet. But I swear I'll get him back for you. We're the Reese brothers, remember? We'll find a way."

"I can't even think anymore." Shaking my head, I cut my gaze to the ground. "I need a timeout. I need all of this to stop for a few minutes so I can figure this out."

Charlotte's voice suddenly infiltrated my mind. *"I need it to stop, Porter."*

I'd only thought I understood her before that day.

But I had no clue the hell she was living through.

And, if I was being honest with myself, a part of my heart was happy for her that she'd found her son.

But why did it have to be *my* son?

"Come on, Porter. I'll drive you home," Dad said.

"I got him," Tanner countered. "You go ahead. Mom's gonna be a wreck. We'll run by my place and grab some clothes, and I'll stay with him tonight."

I nodded absently.

A few minutes later, I found my ass in Tanner's Mercedes, the pitch-black night sky bearing down on me with the weight of a thousand lifetimes.

"When we get to my place, you want to fight the pond?" he asked, his eyes on the road.

"No," I replied, digging the phone from my back pocket.

The police had confiscated it from me when they'd brought me in.

"You hungry?"

"No."

"What about a drink? You want to get sloshed?"

Pressing the power button on my phone, I kept my head down as I answered, "I could drink the entirety of Russia's vodka supply and it wouldn't numb me enough to handle this shit right now."

The light on my phone illuminated the car, and the image on my home screen gutted me. It was a picture of Travis and Hannah. He was smiling directly at the camera, happy and carefree, but she was sitting beside him, gazing up at him like he held the keys to the universe.

My lungs caught fire as I stared at that picture, my hand gripping the phone impossibly tight, as if I could bring that moment to life.

When my phone finished booting up, a million notifications popped up on my screen, blocking Travis's sweet face. Hannah's was still visible off to the side, but I could no longer see her smile. The symbolism wasn't lost on me.

Among the messages was a stream of texts from my mom, probably from when they had first hauled me away. Then some from my dad, one from Tanner, and a handful from the manager at The Porterhouse asking questions about the restaurant, oblivious to the rollercoaster through hell I was currently trapped on.

I scrolled through all of them.

Or almost all of them.

My body turned to stone when I saw her name.

Charlotte: Hey dad I'm with Charlotte she said she will take care of me until you can come get me. I love you. See you soon.

My hand flew out to the side, gripping Tanner's arm. "Stop the car!"

"What?" Tanner asked, jerking his head in my direction.

"Stop the car!" I yelled, hope exploding in my veins. "She's going to give him back."

"What?" he repeated incredulously.

My hands shook, and a huge, manic smile pulled at my lips. "Oh God, she's going to give him back." I pressed on her name and lifted my phone to my ear.

"What the hell are you talking about?" my brother asked.

The ringing of the phone droned in my ear as I explained, "She let Travis text me. Said she'd take care of him until I could get there to pick him up."

When her voicemail picked up, I hit end and then immediately hit send again. It started ringing all over again.

"Porter, stop," Tanner whispered, pulling off to the side of the road.

Her voicemail picked up again, and this time, I decided to leave a message.

"Hey, sweetheart. I just got Travis's text."

"Porter. *Stop*," Tanner urged, trying to grab my phone.

Leaning away, I smacked his hand. "God, baby. What a fucking day." I blew out a hard breath. "I'm on my way now. Tell Travis I love him. Actually...Christ, I love both of you." I paused and lowered my voice. "Stay out of the darkness until I get there, Charlotte. I swear on my life I had no idea he was your son. I promise we'll figure this out." I hit end and dropped the phone into my lap, a renewed faith blazing inside me. "All right. Let's go. She lives up north, near the hospital. I'll tell you how to get there."

Tanner didn't put the car into drive. He sat there, staring at the steering wheel. "She's not just going to give him back to you."

"What the fuck are you talking about? Yes. She is. Here— read the text." I lifted my phone in his direction.

But, when he turned to look at me, his painful gaze was aimed over it. "You heard Mark. They filed an order with the court to keep you away from him."

"So she changed her mind," I argued. "She let him text me, Tanner. That means something."

His jaw was hard as he shook his head. "Yeah. It does. But it could mean a lot of things. Maybe she had a weak moment. Maybe Travis jacked her phone and sent it behind her back. There could be a million different maybes about why she did it. But the only thing I know for sure is that she's *not* giving him back."

The bitterness of anger lit my tongue. "You don't know shit!"

He didn't raise his voice as he said, "I know that she just found her kid after ten years of him being gone. Rita told me she's been living in a haze since he went missing. And, now, she finally got that back." He shrugged. "I'm sorry, but I refuse to believe she's just going to hand him over to you."

He was wrong.

So fucking wrong that rage consumed me.

Fisting the front of his shirt, I yanked him toward me.

"Yes, she will!"

He caught my wrists and squeezed painfully. "I hate it as much as you do, Porter. And I will fight to the ends of the earth to keep him in our family. But that is what we are going to have to do. *Fight.* If you go over there now, screw this up, and end up in jail, where does that leave your chances of getting even part-time custody?"

I gave him a hard shake. "I won't screw this up! She's giving him back."

"Why? Think about it, Porter. Why would she give you *her son*?"

My body coiled tight, twisting the pain and anguish into a violent fury. "Because she has to!" A sob tore from my throat, and I gasped for air. "Because she fucking has to." My voice broke. "I can't live like this. What if he needs me in the middle of the night? What if the call comes for a transplant and I'm not there? I swore to him that I'd take care of him after Catherine died." My shoulders shook uncontrollably. "Tanner, I gave him my word. She *has* to give him back. There's no other option." I shoved off his chest, righting myself in my seat before slamming my fist into the dashboard. "Just fucking take me to her. I can make her understand. I know I can."

His eyebrows pinched together. "And what if she doesn't?"

"Then we'll play it your way and fight it out in the courtroom. But, tonight, I need to see her and get a read on where her head is at. And I need to see him so I can assure him that everything is going to be okay. He's probably fucking terrified."

He sighed and dropped his head back against the

headrest. "It's a bad idea, Porter."

"Maybe. But it's all I got."

"But it's not!" he implored, rolling his head so he was once again facing me. "Mark is the best. If anyone can make a court see why Travis needs you, it's him. You break this protection order and you can kiss that goodbye. You have a shot to stay a part of his life."

"I don't want to be a *part* of his life. I want to be there every fucking day."

"You show up to her place tonight, try to force her to hear you out, you're going to lose him forever. And Christ, Porter? What about Hannah? She needs you at home, not warming a jail cell."

I cringed, my heart breaking at the idea of telling Hannah. "Fuck," I groaned, fisting the top of my hair. "I know. But I can't just go home and wait this out. I have to do something."

"We *are* going to do something. We're going to do so many goddamn somethings these people won't know what hit them. But not like this. You need to play it safe. No calls. No texts. No visits."

I groaned. "I can't."

"You *have* to. First thing in the morning, I'll go on the offense with this and set up a legal team to work on Travis. Meanwhile, you play defense. Keep talking to the police and giving them everything you have on Catherine until we can clear your name."

I dropped my head back against the headrest and stared at the dark sky. "Do you think I have any chance of getting him back?"

"Yeah. I do. Because we're not going to stop until that

happens. I'll call Rita, see if she can take me over there to see him. I'll make sure he knows we love him and put his mind at ease. Okay?"

The knots in my stomach twisted tighter, but I had no choice but to agree. "Yeah. Okay."

FIVE

Charlotte

"YOU NEED TO TRY TO SLEEP," MY MOM WHISPERED, handing me a mug of coffee.

"I know," I replied equally as soft.

I hadn't slept all night. Even with the mental and emotional exhaustion of the day, my body wouldn't settle. It seemed to be a common problem though. Mom and Tom had gone home around three and returned at seven.

I tipped the drink to my lips, propped my shoulder on the doorjamb, and continued to peer into my bedroom at Lucas's form tucked securely under the blankets. It was shortly past nine a.m. and he was still sound asleep.

I could never explain how surreal it had felt to walk into my apartment with my son, his small hand wrapped in mine.

That apartment had been my home for over six years, but suddenly, it felt all wrong. It was too small. Too sterile. Too dark. Too empty.

One look around with eyes no longer shrouded by darkness and I almost didn't want him to be there at all. The other option had been letting him go to Brady's. And there wasn't a chance in hell that was going to happen. The one and only time Brady had mentioned it, I'd immediately shut all conversation down.

I was well aware a one-bedroom apartment wasn't going to cut it. Financially, I had the resources to get a new place. Something nicer. Something bigger. Maybe even a house with a backyard. Though, time was going to be my biggest obstacle.

But no one, not even his father, was going to take my son away from me again.

Thankfully, Brady hadn't pushed the issue. However, he'd made it clear that he would be spending the night on my sofa. I understood. I couldn't tear my eyes off our son, either.

Slowly, Lucas had warmed to Brady. The two of them had spent over an hour on a bench at the police station, Lucas teaching his father the fine art of Minecraft after Brady had downloaded the app on his phone.

Brady and I would never be friends, and nothing would erase the vile things he'd said to me over the years, but seeing him smiling and laughing with our son went a long way to start soothing the wounds.

It had been late when we'd finally been able to leave the police station, and we'd gotten home well after one a.m. But, despite the time, the first thing I'd done was unload the bag of his medications and sort them out. It was a task Lucas was all too willing to help with. Given his age, I was surprised by how much he knew. He'd correctly listed off all of his medicines, dosages (one pill or two), and how often he was supposed to take them (morning, noon, or night).

I loved that he was well educated about his condition.

I hated that he had needed that education at all.

And, with over thirty prescription bottles now filling one of my kitchen cabinets, it was a constant reminder that keeping him might be infinitely harder than getting him back had been.

I had made plans to call his numerous specialists first thing in the morning to schedule meetings and request all of his medical records. I'd been a dedicated physician since the day I'd graduated medical school, but Lucas had just become my most important patient of all.

When his medications were organized, Lucas sat on the couch and regaled my mom and Tom with silly stories about video games and pranks he'd pulled on his private tutors (more people I'd be contacting in the morning.)

So I got busy getting my bedroom ready for him.

I stripped the sheets off the bed that, only one night earlier, Porter and I had shared. I cleared the empty beer bottle he'd left on the nightstand after we'd spent the night laughing and talking, naked and alone in the darkness. His overnight bag was still in the corner, and I fought the urge to lift his shirt to my nose and fill my lungs with the comfort I'd only been able to find in his arms. I shoved it in the closet and shut the door. And, as I erased him from my room, I *pretended* like the thought of him truly being gone wasn't breaking me.

I still had no clue what his role in all of this mess had been. Brady and Tom wouldn't let up about the coincidence of it all.

Though, I was more skeptical.

The first thing I'd learned in medical school was that, when you hear hoof beats, don't automatically assume it's a zebra. It's probably a horse. More often than not, the simplest, most logical answer was usually correct.

I was a pulmonologist.

And Porter had a child with a pulmonary issue.

But, even knowing that, it didn't change our unique situation.

I knew Porter, and there was nothing he wouldn't do to get his son back.

And he knew me, so he had to be aware that there was nothing I wouldn't do to keep him.

We were already at a stalemate, and the match was just getting started.

"Hey," Brady whispered, sidling up behind Mom and me. He rested his palms on our backs and asked, "He still asleep?"

"Yeah," I replied, curling the mug of coffee into my chest.

"He had to be exhausted," Mom added.

"Susan, you mind if I have a minute alone with Charlotte?"

Her gaze flicked to mine in question, and I gave her a short nod.

Crossing her arms over her chest, she looked to Brady and asked, "Are you going to be an asshole?"

Yep. That was my mom.

Brady chuckled. "Wasn't planning on it."

"Then I suppose I can give you two a minute. You want some coffee?"

"I'd love some," he replied, a small smile playing at his lips.

"Okay, then. Be nice and don't make me hurt either one of you on such a joyous day." Pressing up onto her toes, she

44

pecked my cheek and then patted Brady on the chest before strolling away.

Brady moved to fill her empty space in the doorway. "Are you doing okay?"

"Yeah. Of course," I answered. "What about you?"

His green eyes warmed. "It's weird. Ya know? He's my son, but he's also this little stranger."

"I know. I get nervous every time he so much as looks at me," I confessed and immediately felt awkward about it. "I mean—"

"He looks a lot more like you than I was expecting. In all the age progression photos they made over the years, he always looked like me."

I smiled and swallowed hard. "He's got your chin."

He chuckled and scrubbed his jaw. "Poor guy."

I took another sip and turned my attention back to Lucas, allowing the silence to linger between us. Though there was nothing comfortable about it.

"Thank you," Brady rasped.

With wide eyes, I snapped my gaze to his. "For what?"

He cleared his throat. "I felt like I was going to die this morning when you had to give him that breathing treatment thing. I literally couldn't breathe the whole time."

I patted his arm. "Hey, it's okay. He's fine now."

"You jumped right in, while I stood there, paralyzed by fear that I'd just gotten him back and I was already going to lose him again." His voice cracked as he covered his mouth.

"Brady," I whispered, my chest tightening. "That's my job. It's different for me. I'll teach you. It won't be so scary next time."

He nodded. "I don't want there to be a next time."

"I don't either, but unfortunately, there are going to be *a lot* of next times. He's sick, Brady. *Really* sick."

He hooked his arm around my shoulders and gathered me into his side. My body was stiff, but I allowed him the contact.

But it was all for him.

What I wouldn't have given for it to be Porter's strong arm. His reassuring words in my ear. His lips pressing into the top of my hair. His warmth enveloping me.

As though he could read my mind, Brady said, "I know, which is why we need to talk about Porter Reese."

My heart lurched. Stepping away from his side, I caught the doorknob. Silently pulling the door shut, I left Lucas peacefully sleeping inside.

"What about him?" I asked.

"I don't want my son having anything to do with that asshole."

And just like that, our moment was gone.

I rolled my eyes and crossed my arms over my chest. "Jesus Christ, how many times are we going to have this conversation? I agreed to the protection order, didn't I?"

"You did." He took an ominous step toward me. "But then, an hour later, you let our son text that man."

My back shot straight. "How do you know that?"

"The same way I know that Porter was blowing your phone up in the middle of the night."

Now, that was news to me. I had no idea where my phone was. When I'd last seen it, it was on the end table in the living room. But, after Lucas had woken up having difficulty breathing, I'd lost track of basically everything else. Clearly,

Brady had not.

"You went through my phone?" I hissed.

He cocked his head to the side and leveled me with a scowl. "Tell me you understand."

"You went through my fucking phone?" I semi-repeated, stepping forward until we were nose to nose.

My mom suddenly appeared between us. "No way. Break it up, you two. We are not doing this today." She took my coffee from my hand when I refused to back down.

"Say it, Charlotte," Brady demanded.

"You had no right!" I snapped.

"And neither did you. He's *our* son. Both of ours. You do not get to make decisions by yourself."

"Hey. Hey. Hey," Tom said, wading into what was about to escalate into World War III. "Enough."

Brady and I continued our stare down around them, neither of us willing to concede.

Ultimately, it was a knock at the door that finally broke the tension.

With my teeth clenched, I dragged my gaze away from Brady and marched to the door. My footsteps were almost as heavy as the anger brewing inside me.

I snatched the door open and then froze.

Topaz-blue eyes.

Short, blond hair.

Strong jaw covered in scruff.

Bright, white smile.

"Hi," he said softly.

My mouth dried and everything slowed, tears I should have long since run out of filling my eyes.

47

It wasn't Porter. But he looked close enough to cause my heart to splinter.

"Oh, honey," Rita said, gliding past Tanner and wrapping me in a hug. "You should have called."

"I…uh…" I stammered, my eyes still locked on Tanner.

Secretly, I flashed my gaze over his shoulder, searching—and hoping—for any sign of Porter. There was none.

And, when Brady's presence hit my back, I was suddenly relieved.

"You are not here right now," he growled at Tanner.

Tanner kept staring at me. His handsome smile, which matched his brother's, never faltered as he stated, "I brought some of Travis's things."

Brady cut around me and snatched the bag from his hands. "Leave."

"Oh, give it a rest," Rita snapped at Brady. Then her tone became sweet as she asked me, "How are you doing, honey?"

I kept staring at Tanner as I bit my lip and shook my head.

"You overwhelmed?" she whispered.

I sucked in a sharp breath and nodded.

She palmed either side of my face. "Well, don't you worry. I'm here now." Then she was gone.

Or, more accurately, she was now gone from my face and up in Brady's.

"All right. Listen up. Tanner was just leaving. I, however—"

She didn't get to finish what was probably going to be an amazing speech because she was interrupted by the sound of a little boy's glee-filled shriek.

"Uncle Tan!"

"Fuck," Brady growled and started to turn toward him.

Snaking a hand out, I caught his elbow. "Don't you dare!"

"Charlotte," he warned.

"His world has been flipped upside down. Let him have these few minutes of comfort. I'll toe the line about Porter after this. But he's already seen Tanner. You are *not* taking this away from him."

For several beats, he scowled at me, but he finally tipped his chin and stepped to the side, allowing Lucas room to get to the man he'd grown up thinking was his uncle.

Our boy didn't slow until he crashed into Tanner's front.

I'd only met Tanner Reese once. So I wasn't exactly an expert on his repertoire of expressions. But there was no mistaking the tangible pain that flickered through his features before he was able to conceal them with a smile.

"Hey, Trav," he murmured.

God. I was so sick of my heart hurting all the time. But it did. At every turn.

And it seemed I wasn't the only one. Porter would be destroyed. But his whole family had been affected too.

"What are you doing here?" Lucas asked, craning his head back, his eyes sparkling with tears. "Did Dad come with you?"

Tanner squatted low and wrapped him into a hug. One so deep that even I felt the love packed inside it. "No. I'm sorry." He lowered his voice. "He told me to tell you that he loves you so much and that he'll see you as soon as he can."

Brady scoffed beside me, and I swung a scathing glare his way.

He shrugged, completely unfazed.

"Can you stay?" Lucas asked, his excitement palpable.

Tanner's gaze flicked to mine in question.

Covering my mouth, I shook my head, guilt churning my stomach.

"Sorry, bud. I can't. I need to get to work," he lied.

My nose started stinging, and I cut my eyes away so no one would be able to see if any tears actually escaped.

"Okay," Lucas breathed, his disappointment palpable. "Will you tell Dad I love him? And Hannah. Oh, and make sure she's not messing with my Legos."

Tanner's face once again crumbled, his smile unable to mask it. "Sure thing."

"Oh! And Nana. Will you tell her that Charlotte's good at the nebulizer? She's, like, a doctor and stuff. Oh, and Grandpa. Tell him he's not allowed to go fishing until I get home. He'll catch all the good ones without me."

My lungs burned as the air became toxic.

He truly believed he was going home.

"Yeah!" Tanner exclaimed, rising to his full height at the same time a tear finally made it out of his eye. He wiped it on his shoulder and kept right on smiling. "Dude, I won't let him anywhere near the pond. I promise."

"Okay, good," he whispered.

Tanner tucked him against his legs, patting his back as he whispered, "Love you, Trav."

"Love you, too," he mumbled, releasing his uncle. The devastation on my son's face was staggering.

"Come on, my man," Brady said, taking his hand, leading him into the house, and then shutting the door behind them.

The minute it clicked, Tanner lost it.

"Jesus," he hissed. He rested his hands on his head and paced a small circle. "This is so fucked up. Tell me you know this is fucked up, Charlotte."

"Tanner, it's not her fault," Rita soothed.

"What do you expect me to do?" I asked.

Tanner stopped, planted a hand on his hip, and aimed a pointed finger at the door. "I want you to remember what it felt like the day he was taken from you. Because that is exactly what you are doing to Porter right now."

"I can't worry about Porter!" I cried. "He's my son."

Tanner scoffed and stared at me in disbelief. "Okay. Then I want you to think about *your son*. Remember the day he was taken from *you*? Now, I want you to imagine you are an eleven—or as it turns out ten—year-old boy and your entire family has been snatched from you. Because that is what you have done to him."

I sucked in a ragged breath. "This is an impossible situation. I don't have the answers."

"His name is Travis. Or Lucas. Or whatever the hell you want to call him. But *he* is the answer. This isn't about my family or yours. Nor is it about you or Porter. It is about that little boy who is now caught in the middle of all of us."

Words. More fucking *words.*

All of them the truth.

"I don't know what to do!"

"Do what's right!" he exclaimed. Turning his gaze on Rita, he softened his voice. "I'm sorry. But you know it's true."

"Go!" she ordered, wrapping her arms around me. "Shit. Charlotte. I'm so sorry. I did not know he was going to unload on you like that or I never would have brought him."

"He's right," I mumbled.

"No, he's not. He's your son, honey. You deserve some

time to figure all of this out without him acting like a prick."

My stomach rolled as I watched Tanner walk away, his gait a little too similar to his brother's.

"I need to confess something, and you can't tell anyone else," I whispered.

"Okay, yeah. Anything."

"I miss Porter," I choked out.

"Oh, honey. It's not wrong to miss him."

"But everyone keeps telling me it is. They're convinced he knew about Lucas. Brady won't let up. And Tom somehow even managed to get Mom on the bandwagon."

"Charlotte, look at me." Using my shoulders, she forced me away until she caught my gaze. "Brady just needs somebody to blame. He's been doing that to you for ten years. Now, he's doing it to Porter. He's an asshole. Assholes do that."

I half laughed, half sobbed.

"And Tom," she continued. "He's basically your father. Hell, he's even sleeping with your mom."

"Ew!"

She smiled. "Somebody hurt his baby, and for ten years, he couldn't figure out who. Now, he thinks he knows. So he is not delaying in extracting his vengeance in your honor."

"I don't need vengeance. I need Porter. He'd know all the right things to say to Lucas. He'd stand up to Brady. Tell Tom to take a fucking hike. He'd even be able to keep Mom from swirling herself into a tizzy."

"Really?" she drawled in surprise. "Porter would do all that? That man does not strike me as an alpha."

I half laughed, half sobbed again, and this time, it turned into all-out tears. "He'd do it for me."

Her arms tightened around my shoulders. "Then that's all that matters. Give it some time, Char. It's been one day. Stop looking at the big picture and look at the now.

So what… Brady is being a dick. Tom is being overprotective. Your mom is trying to take care of the world. Really, it's just another day for you." She patted my chest over my heart. "Focus on what matters in here. Right now, Lucas is inside, and Tanner I'm sure is going home to let Porter know that he's okay. So stop stressing yourself out with the rest of it. It's all going to fall into place."

I wasn't sure I agreed with her.

But she definitely wasn't wrong.

I flashed her a tight smile. "He wants us to call him Travis."

She smiled back and patted my heart again. "Yeah, but he's always going to be Lucas in here."

SIX

Charlotte

"CAN I GET YOU SOMETHING TO DRINK?" BRADY'S WIFE, Stephanie, asked as she opened the front door for me. Her long, curly, blond hair hung over her shoulders, and their son, William, was clawing at the ringlets like they were his favorite toy.

"I'm good. Thanks," I replied, walking toward Brady, who was peering into the backyard from his recliner.

It had almost killed me, but I'd dropped Lucas off at Brady's long enough for me to go to my office and pass off all of my patient files to Laughlin. It was official. For the first time in ten years, I was taking some time off. Six weeks to be exact. Greg had teased me that it was like I was going on maternity leave, and in a lot of ways, he had been right. I needed time to build a relationship and a bond with my son, and nothing— not even my job—was going to prevent me from making up for lost time.

Well, that's not totally true. The surprise party of sorts in the conference room definitely took a few minutes of my time. They had cake and sparkling grape juice. Everyone was smiling and congratulating me on not only getting my son back, but taking time off to spend with him. Meanwhile, I stared at the minute hand on the clock, wondering how many gift cards I would have to purchase in order not to feel bad about making an early exit.

"Have you seen this?" Brady asked, passing me a newspaper.

I glanced outside at Lucas and breathed a sigh of relief that he was still there. I was convinced that he was going to disappear again. Every morning, my heart raced as I climbed off my makeshift bed on the couch and hurried down the hall to the bedroom he'd taken over as his own.

Every morning, he'd been there.

Every morning, I expected that to change.

"Seen what?" I asked.

"Your boyfriend has apparently decided to petition the courts for full custody."

My body grew tight. "Full custody?"

"That's what it says," Brady replied, tipping his chin toward the paper. "I left a message on Paul's voicemail to see if he's formally heard anything from Porter's attorney. But, according to The Post, that's his goal."

"No fucking way," I breathed, picking the newspaper up and scanning the article, unsuccessfully avoiding the picture of Porter, Tanner, and Lucas huddled together at a Braves game.

Much like they had the day he had been kidnapped, the

media had caught wind of Lucas's return.

Magically over the last six days, a barrage of pictures of the Reese family had surfaced and started circulating around social media. And, considering that Tanner Reese was a household name, people didn't take kindly to the idea of his nephew being kept from him.

Judgmental Judys from all over the world started taking sides with people they had never met, all of them gearing up for a down-and-dirty custody battle over an innocent child. I'd never been more ashamed of the human race as I was while reading the hateful and disgusting comments on the one and only article I'd read online about our situation.

Half of them blasting me.

Half of them blasting Porter.

All of them uninformed.

I kept my eyes aimed at Brady and asked, "He can't do this, right?"

He rested his elbows on his knees, steepling his fingers under his chin, and stated smugly, "You finally ready to listen to me now?"

I pinned him with a glower. "You can stop being an ass. He hasn't had any contact with Porter."

And he hadn't. Lucas asked for Porter more often than not. It had killed, but I'd made up excuses. I'd promised Brady I'd toe the line about contact with Porter, and until the investigation was concluded, I had every intention of keeping my end of the bargain.

"What about Tanner?" Brady shot back. "Any more contact there?"

"It was only that once, and that wasn't my choice. Lucas

had already seen him. I wasn't going to drag him kicking and screaming away."

"You're his parent, Charlotte. Until he's eighteen, everything he does is our choice."

I looked back to Lucas, playing with a remote-control helicopter my mom had bought him. His eyes were aimed toward the sky, a huge smile covering his face.

In the six days since we'd gotten him back, I'd seen him smile numerous times, but never like that. His eyes were always cautious, and he wore a permanent mask of unease. But, right then, he had not a care in the world except for getting that brown-and-tan-camo helicopter to stay in the air.

The minute his gaze would find mine or Brady's, his smile would disappear. Most of the time, he covered it quickly, plastering a new grin on before we had the chance to question it. But, each and every time, for those three seconds, his mask faltered and revealed his true emotions—and they were heartbreaking.

"Tanner's harmless," I said to Brady.

"Oh, really?" He scoffed. "You think it's Porter paying for three new big-wig attorneys and a publicist to spin this whole bullshit social media campaign their way?"

I threw my arms out to my sides. "I don't fucking know. Okay? I've never done this before."

"None of us have! But a little common sense would go a long fucking way."

I glared at him. "I've kept my word. He hasn't talked to Porter or anyone else in the Reese family since that first day. You can lay off, okay? He's not getting full custody."

He barked a humorless laugh. "No. Charlotte, he's not.

Because there isn't a chance in hell that he's getting *any* custody of my son. If that asshole and his stupid fucking brother think they can march into that courtroom and try to take what's mine, they're in for the surprise of their lives. I did not spend ten years searching to turn my son over to the man who kidnapped him."

"He didn't kidnap him!" I snapped. "Christ, Brady. Even Tom has admitted Porter had nothing to do with that woman taking him."

The aura around him suddenly became dense. He had been pissed before, but with those four *words*, he'd become damn near livid. He took only two steps, but there was no mistaking his movements as anything other than a malicious prowl.

Keeping his voice low, he seethed, "Just because he didn't physically take him doesn't mean he didn't spend years keeping our son from us. I don't know what the fuck that sick piece of shit did to brainwash you, but for over a month, our son stood right in front of you while you chose not to see him. You want to act like you still don't see him. Fine. But I do. And I won't stop until that man is out of Lucas's life forever."

My mouth gaped open, his words slashing through me with a vicious velocity. Brady had said a lot of nasty things to me over the years. Most of which were true, so I couldn't even argue with him.

But this? This was by far his lowest blow.

"You think I should have recognized Lucas the first time I saw him?" I asked, awestruck.

His jaw ticked as he held my gaze, screaming his confirmation when he hadn't uttered a single word.

"Holy shit. You do," I whispered, anger and shock swirling inside me. My body hummed as I sneered, "There's no pleasing you, is there? He's finally home. I'm working with you, against my better judgment, to keep him away from the only man he's ever trusted. And that *still* isn't good enough for you."

"See, that's the problem, Charlotte. As we've found out over the last ten years, your judgment is shit. Porter Reese will never be a part of my son's life." He pointed a single finger in my face. "Do not cross me on this. That is your only warning."

Like hackles, the hairs on the back of my neck stood on end. "My warning?"

"Don't push—"

Suddenly, the door slid open and Lucas appeared, preventing me from a lifetime in prison for having killed his father.

"Hey, Charlotte," he called cheerfully.

Keeping my death glare on Brady, I replied, "Hey, Travis. You ready to go?"

"Sure," he chirped. "Hey, guess what? Brady gave me a twenty-dollar iTunes card so I can buy some new skins for my character in Minecraft."

"Wow. That was really nice of him," I said in a sugary-sweet tone that would have made Rita proud, all the while continuing my stare down with the devil.

"I'll go grab my stuff," he said, taking off down the hall.

When I was sure he was out of earshot, I snarled, "Don't you dare threaten me. I've spent a lot of years being your doormat, but I'm done, Brady. You want to make idle threats? You better be prepared to back them up. And *that* is your only warning."

His lips curled into a sardonic smile. "Right." Though the way he said it sounded a whole lot more like, *Fuck you.*

He casually walked away, seemingly unfazed. Meanwhile, my pulse was thundering in my ears.

I was so fucking done with Brady's bullshit.

Though, after that little showdown, I had a feeling it was just getting started.

<hr />

It was eleven that same night and I was finally going through the bag of clothes my mom had bought for me to wear to the custody hearing the following day. None of them were anything I ever would have picked out for myself. They were all too pink. Too lacy. Too floral. But, then again, I could hardly wear a scrub top to court. After tossing them aside, I took a sip of my glass of wine. I'd poured it under the pretense of celebrating my first night of vacation from work, but I was truly drinking it to calm my nerves.

Between Porter's new attempt to get full custody and Brady's being even more of a dick than usual, I'd been a mess all afternoon.

On one hand, I shouldn't have been surprised by Brady. A few kind moments since we'd gotten Lucas back did not equal a changed man. I should have expected he'd slide back down the asshole ladder. Though, if I really thought about it, he'd never truly climbed off.

Porter though? He'd shocked me. And more than that? He'd hurt me.

It was stupid. We were fighting over the most prized possession a person could ever have. All bets were off. But maybe that was exactly the problem. Lucas/Travis wasn't a possession at all.

He was a confused little boy who, as much as it pained me, should have a say over his life. And he'd made it abundantly clear that he wanted Porter.

Only hours earlier, I'd sat outside of his door, listening to him cry tears he would never show me, after I'd told him that he couldn't call his dad until the courts said it was okay.

His face had crumbled, in turn crumbling my soul.

I hated it for him.

I hated it for me.

And, secretly, I hated it for Porter as well.

After picking my phone up, I brought up the thread of messages I shared with Porter. That picture of us laughing in bed was still front and center. My pulse spiked at the sight.

I traced my fingers over the strong curve of his jaw, wishing I could feel the scruff that had once sent chills down my spine.

My eyes drifted to Travis's message to his dad.

Hey dad I'm with Charlotte she said she will take care of me until you can come get me. I love you. See you soon.

It wasn't quite what I had told him when I'd let him send that text, but I assumed it was what his eager mind had heard.

Porter hadn't responded, which honestly had surprised the hell out of me. There was an order of protection in place, but he wasn't the type of guy who would just walk away and hope for the best. By now, I figured he'd be beating down my door.

Closing my eyes, I clutched my phone tight.

That afternoon, when we'd gotten home from Brady's, Lucas and I had watched a movie on my laptop.

Well, more accurately, he'd watched a movie on my laptop. I'd watched him.

He was so much like Porter it was insane. Honest to God, he even looked like him in a lot of ways. In the great debate of nature versus nurture, Lucas was proof that nurture always won out.

I had to stop obsessing about Porter. It wasn't doing any of us any good. It was crushing me more with every passing minute. And, honestly, it was distracting me from what truly mattered: having my son back.

Clicking on Porter's name in my contacts, I had every intention of deleting him from my phone. Only my fingers froze, hovering in midair over the screen.

Unblock this number stared up at me like a neon sign.

Unblock.

Unblock.

Un-fucking-block.

My mouth dried, and anger lit my veins.

I'd never blocked Porter's number.

But I could guess who had. The same man who had gone through my phone and read my text messages. The same man who, only hours earlier, had warned me not to cross him.

"I'm gonna fucking kill him," I breathed, pressing the magical unblock button.

And then my heart stopped as a voicemail notification popped up on my screen, Porter's name in the bubble.

I immediately hit play, chills pebbling my skin as his

deep, desperate voice filled my ear, "Hey, sweetheart. I just got Travis's text."

"Porter. *Stop*," Tanner said in the background.

"Please don't stop," I whispered, gnawing on my bottom lip.

"God, baby. What a fucking day," Porter said before releasing a hard exhale into the phone. "I'm on my way now. Tell Travis I love him. Actually...Christ, I love both of you."

I slapped a hand over my mouth.

But Porter from days ago continued in my ear, his voice taking on a low, familiar rumble, "Stay out of the darkness until I get there, Charlotte. I swear on my life I had no idea he was your son. I promise we'll figure this out."

The message ended, but with burning lungs, I pressed play again.

"Hey, sweetheart. I just got Travis's message..."

I stood up and began to pace, my chest constricting as he said, "Actually...Christ, I love both of you."

When the message ended, I pressed play again. This time focusing on a different sentence.

"I swear on my life I had no idea he was your son."

Thirteen words.

And call me naïve, stupid, or whatever, but I believed every single one of them.

I pressed play again.

And then again.

And again.

And again.

Over and over until I couldn't breathe around the lump in my throat.

I wasn't sure what had changed and why he hadn't shown up that night. Probably the protection order Brady had so adamantly sworn we needed.

Brady.

Brady.

Fucking Brady.

SEVEN

Porter

"WHAT DO YOU THINK TRAVIS'S FRIEND'S HOUSE LOOKS like?" Hannah asked as I unbuckled her from her car seat.

"I don't know, baby."

"How many sleeps until he comes home?"

Sighing, I put her on my hip and headed up the sidewalk to my parents' front door. "I don't know."

It made me a coward, but I'd chickened out on telling her the truth about Travis. She wouldn't have understood. Instead, I told her that he was staying with a friend for a little bit. She'd asked approximately seven million questions in the week since he'd been gone, each one slicing me to the quick. Eventually, I'd have to tell her the truth. But, hopefully, not today.

"Does his friend have a TV in his room?" she chirped.

"I don't know."

"Can I have a TV in my room?"

I grinned down at her. "No."

My stomach was in knots, and my nerves had left me with jitters all morning, but she always managed to make me smile. She was the only thing that had kept me going over the last week.

My mom swung the front door open before I had the chance to knock. Clapping her hands together, she reached for Hannah. "There's my girl."

"Nana!" Hannah squealed, diving from my arms. "Guess what? Travis's friend has a TV in his bedroom."

Mom arched an eyebrow at me. "Oh, *he* does?"

I shrugged and stepped forward to kiss my mom's temple. "I have no idea. Where's Tanner?"

"Right here," he said, rounding the corner, wearing a tailor-made navy-blue suit.

"Hey, Uncle Tan."

He winked and moved closer to tickle her. "Hey, beautiful."

She giggled wildly.

Catching his bicep, I dragged him into the dining room.

"Hey, hey, hey. Don't wrinkle the suit," he complained.

I flashed my gaze back to Hannah, who was prattling on about God only knew what, but my mom's nervous, blue eyes were leveled on me. I shot her a placating smile and then gave her my back.

"Full custody?" I seethed at my brother. "Have you fucking lost your mind?"

"Relax. Kurt knows what he's doing."

Tanner had brought in three of the best attorneys in the country to work with Mark. Seriously, when my brother set his mind on something, he went from zero to a million in one point five seconds. As far as he was concerned, what was supposed to be a preliminary custody hearing quickly became the likes of the OJ Simpson trial.

I'd begged him to keep it all on the down low, but where Tanner went, so did the media.

But, even though I appreciated his support, I was done with the fanfare. I wanted my son back and not to have our laundry aired out for the entire world.

"Fuck Kurt. This is ridiculous, and I can't handle it. Screaming that I'm trying to take him away from Charlotte and Brady isn't going to win me any sympathy. Full custody is a threat. And, if you or Kurt think otherwise, you're clearly not a parent."

His eyebrows shot up. I hoped it was because he was starting to understand, but more likely, it was because he could tell I was on the verge of a nervous breakdown.

"Okay, okay. We'll tell Kurt to back down," he assured. "Just take a deep breath and try to stay positive."

Oh, I was positive.

Positive I was losing my mind.

Positive I needed to get my son back.

Positive Catherine had fucked me from beyond the grave.

Keeping all of that to myself, I drew in a deep breath and cracked my neck.

"Better," he praised. Then he straightened my tie. "I'm impressed. You look almost human."

I'd barely been surviving over the last week. I'd spent almost every day at the police station, "cooperating" with the investigation. Which really just meant I was spending my days sitting in a room while they scoured through my past and searched for a reason to arrest me. So far, the truth had successfully kept me out of a pair of cuffs. But I hadn't slept more than a handful of hours over the last seven days. I was tired, physically and emotionally, and I missed my son something fierce.

But the days kept going without me.

Sunrise.

Sunset.

Wash. Rinse. Repeat.

I swatted Tanner's hand away. "I don't feel human."

He patted my shoulder. "Well, let's hope today changes that."

There wasn't enough hope in the world for how much I *needed* today to change it.

"Dad!" Tanner shouted, strutting to where Mom was still standing at the front door. "Let's go. We're pulling out."

Dad came barreling down the stairs. "I'm coming. I'm coming. Quit your yelling."

He paused for only a second to kiss Mom and tickle Hannah's neck before we were all out the door and heading to Tanner's Mercedes.

"Keep me updated!" Mom called after us. "Love you!"

"Love you too!" we all yelled back in unison, climbing into the car.

I rubbed my sweaty palms on my thighs and asked, "Have you heard from Rita?"

His eyes caught mine in the rearview mirror. "She's still not talking to me."

"Shit," I breathed, fighting the urge to rake a hand through my hair. I'd spent thirty minutes styling it, doing my best to look like I had it all together while I was falling apart.

Dad turned in his seat. "Have you talked to Mark?"

"At least seven hundred and fifty times," I answered, shifting in my seat, unable to sit still.

"And what's the latest?"

"There is no latest. The protection order is still in place. And me getting any kind of custody is basically the long shot of the century. And probably smaller than that now that Kurt has announced I'm petitioning for full custody." I peered out the window, my throat on fire.

My dad reached back and patted my leg. "It's gonna work out, Porter. Have a little faith. You're a good dad. Travis loves you. The judge will see that."

"And if he doesn't?"

"Hey!" Tanner interrupted. "Don't turn into Pity Porter back there. This is going to happen. End of story. Remember when we first found out about his heart? There was only one option. This is no different."

I nodded and went back to staring out the window. Optimism wasn't exactly my strong suit anymore.

We rode in silence the rest of the way to the courthouse. It wasn't the comfortable silence Charlotte and I shared. It was merely the deceptive lull before the hurricane.

Reaching into my pocket, I felt the crinkled edges of that familiar cocktail napkin I'd tucked in there before we left. The one I'd drawn on what felt like an eternity ago—that silly map that had shown her how to escape the restaurant on our first date. And there I was, weeks later, preparing to go head-to-head with her over the custody of my son.

Her son.

But not *our* son.

What I wouldn't have given for someone to draw me a map so I could escape this hell.

Twenty minutes later, after we'd parked, passed through the metal detectors, and made it into the courthouse, Mark, Kurt, and two other fancy-ass attorneys I mentally referred to as TweedleDee and TweedleDumb met us outside of a courtroom that wasn't nearly big enough for the decision being made inside it.

"How you holding up, Porter?" Mark asked.

I shook his outstretched hand and answered honestly. "I'm not."

"Well, let's see if we can fix that. You ready?"

My nerves ignited. "Not at all. But I guess it's now or never."

Dad cupped my shoulder, and Tanner patted my back.

Shaking my arms out, I prepared for war.

Mark opened the door to courtroom C, and then, on legs that felt as though they were filled with lead, I made my way inside flanked by my legal team.

I wasn't two steps through the door before my desperate gaze found her.

My body locked up tight, but I somehow managed to keep my legs moving.

I couldn't see her face. She was sitting at the table in the front of the room, Brady beside her. Her shoulders were hunched forward, and his fingers—all of which I wanted to break—were splayed across her back.

As if she could read my mind, she roughly shrugged his hand away.

It had only been a week since I'd seen her, but she somehow looked different.

She was wearing a short-sleeve, silk, peach-colored blouse. *Peach.* Fucking ridiculous. My Charlotte wouldn't have been caught dead in anything other than black. But I had to remind myself that her dreams had come true. Maybe she was a different woman now.

Her hair was down, long and straight. At least that was the same. And I almost smiled when she nervously pulled it up into a ponytail only to release it. She did this a lot.

It was how I knew she was winding herself up.

And how I had known when to step in and take her hand, giving her something else to focus on.

My hands twitched to do just that.

I moved on autopilot as my attorneys guided me to a table at the front of the room, my gaze glued to her back, begging her to give me her eyes.

My dad and Tanner filed into the row of chairs behind us, but I kept watching her.

Through it all, the room carried on around us. People rising. A judge entering. People sitting. Our attorneys spoke in jargon I didn't understand. Her attorney whispered in her ear. Brady wrote something on a notepad and then showed it to her. She shoved it away without even reading it.

But she never looked in my direction.

"Mr. Reese," the judge called, snapping my attention off her.

"Yes. Right here." I shot to my feet. Why? I didn't know. It just seemed like I should be standing when they ripped the rug out from underneath me.

"Have a seat, son," he stated, his round belly showing beneath his black robe.

"Right." I glanced at Charlotte, but she was staring straight ahead, her profile unreadable.

"It seems we have a unique situation here," he stated.

I gave the judge my sole attention. "Yes, sir."

"Then you know this is going to take some time to figure all this out."

I nodded. "I do understand that. And I'm okay with that as long as I'm allowed to spend time with my son while we do that."

"That's where we're going to have trouble. I'm sorry, Mr. Reese—"

An icy panic crept through my extremities and into my chest. "It's not his fault," I interrupted. "Travis. It's not his fault that Catherine kidnapped him. It's not his fault that he grew up without his parents." I swung a hand out, motioning to Charlotte. "But I do believe it should be his choice who he wants to live with."

Brady shot to his feet, leaning forward on his knuckles as he exclaimed, "He's ten! He doesn't get to decide."

"Mr. Boyd," the judge warned.

I ignored his outburst. "He would choose me, sir. Every time. I love my son. I've done everything in my power to give him a life despite his health issues and the trauma the woman he thought was his mother cowardly inflicted on us all."

"Bullshit," Brady snarled. "You didn't do shit. Where the hell were you when that whack job was driving my son off a fucking bridge?"

"Brady!" Charlotte scolded.

The judge slammed his gavel and called for order.

But there was none to be found.

Not in a situation like that.

Not when three parents were willing to fight to the death over one innocent child.

I slapped a hard hand on my chest, grinding my teeth together as I seethed, "I was in that fucking water saving him!"

Mark stepped in front of me. "Shut up. You aren't helping your case with this."

"He could have been killed!" Brady continued.

"I'm the only reason he's alive! And I want him back!" I roared.

"You'll never see him again!" he swore as one of the uniformed officers tried to force him to sit down, another getting in my face.

Reluctantly, I quieted, but Tanner took my place.

"You want to point fingers? Where the hell were you the day he was taken in the first place?"

"No!" I yelled at Tanner, shooting back to my feet. I swung my gaze to Charlotte. She was still facing forward, but her body was rigid and her mouth had fallen open. "That was no one's fault. That was all Catherine."

"Calm down or you're all spending the night in a cell!" the judge ordered.

But I couldn't calm down. He was going to take Travis away from me for good. I could feel it in my bones. I was losing him. The car was sinking. His heart was failing. And I was once again fighting the impossible.

I looked at Brady. "Don't do this. This is a crazy situation that we've all been forced into. Emotions are running high.

But I swear, if given the chance, I'm confident that the three of us can work out something in the best interest of our son."

"My son!" Brady roared. "He is not yours."

"Who does he call dad, asshole?" Tanner shouted.

The judge banged his gavel, the sound echoing in my heart.

"No. No. No." I extended my arms out to my sides, my palms up, desperate to stop the chaos before it was too late. "Stop! Please, just…" I closed my eyes, the defeat paralyzing me.

The gavel kept banging.

Brady kept yelling.

Tanner kept replying.

My heart kept beating.

And the world just kept spinning.

Opening my eyes, I found the only person in the room who could possibly understand. Finally, she was staring straight at me, her soft lips parted while guilt and apology lingered in her beautiful features.

And then I said the familiar words she had once begged of me. "I need it to stop."

Her eyes grew wide and her body jerked as though I'd hit her from across the room.

Mark stepped into my space, frantically trying to silence me, but I leaned around him to keep her in my line of sight and shouted to be sure she heard me over the chaos.

"Charlotte, please! I need it to stop!"

She slapped a shaking hand over her mouth, tears sparkling in her eyes.

"Sit down and shut up," Mark growled, shoving me into

my chair.

I went down, but I kept my gaze on Charlotte, pleading with her without the use of words.

Tears rolled off her chin as she started talking to her attorney, her mouth moving a million miles an hour, a pointed finger swinging in my direction.

Hope swelled in my chest.

Still arguing, Tanner and Brady were both dragged from the room, their yells turning into murmurs as the doors closed behind them.

And then everything fell silent. Eerily so.

The judge swept a pointed scowl through the room. "Anyone want to join them?"

"No, your honor," Mark answered for me.

Charlotte answered a little differently. "Can I please say something?"

My heart exploded.

The judge lifted his hand to silence her. "Thank you, Ms. Mills, but I've heard enough."

"Wait...please." Her panicked gaze slipped to mine.

"Enough," he shot back, and Charlotte slowly sank into her chair, defeated.

That same defeat made my gut sour.

Fuck. Fuck. Fuck.

He cleared his throat and then trained his unhappiness on me. "As I was saying, I'm sorry, Mr. Reese, but I can't make a decision on custody *at this time*. From what I've been told, the police are still in the process of concluding their investigation. Once you have been cleared of all involvement, we can proceed. This is a very rare case unlike any I've ever dealt with before. So, before I make any decisions, I'd like to meet with Lucas Boyd personally. I'll also be assigning a Guardian Ad Litem to the case. He or she will be contacting each of you individually, including Mr. Boyd, to conduct interviews and home visits, collect background information, and so forth. In the meantime, the order of protection will remain in place."

My body tensed, and I opened my mouth to object but didn't get a sound out.

"Quiet, Mr. Reese. We'll reconvene in two weeks. And if at that point you've been cleared, we can discuss supervised visitation in the short term until I'm able to make a final ruling."

My chest collapsed, my shoulders rolling forward to combat the pain. Two weeks felt like an insult. It had already been seven agonizing days. The uncertainty of it all was slowly bleeding me dry.

The judge continued talking, the attorneys chiming in to ask questions and set up dates, but I zoned out.

Any hopes I'd had for that day had been crushed.

Yet, when I lifted my head, my eyes once again found hers.

Her dark browns, which had once housed our shared darkness, now blazed with light.

"Two weeks," she mouthed.

"I can't," I mouthed back.

"I promise I'll take care of him." She smiled, and I swear it hit me like a sledgehammer.

But it broke me in all the right places.

Flicking my gaze down, I mouthed, "I hate your shirt."

Her smile grew, tears spilling from her eyes. "Me too."

My chest warmed, and for the first time in over a week, the world slowed.

She hadn't been able to stop it. But the realization that, in some way, shape, or form, we were still on the same team, did more for me than anything else that day.

"Mr. Reese," the judge called. "Do you understand?"

I glanced at Mark, who was glaring at me, clearly unimpressed with Charlotte's shirt as well—or perhaps the fact that we were chatting from opposite tables in the middle of a custody hearing. Whatever.

"Yes, sir. Two weeks," I replied.

EIGHT

Charlotte

BRADY AND I DROVE HOME FROM THE COURTHOUSE IN silence.

Or, at least, I was silent.

Brady talked profusely.

Mainly, he was bitching. Complaining about the judge, the attorney, the bailiff, whoever. Then he went off on a full-blown rant, first about Porter before sparing a few F-bombs for Tanner too.

I ignored all of this.

I was plotting. And not Brady's untimely demise, though the thought had crossed my mind.

No. I was plotting how I was going to finally take my life back.

Just that morning, as I'd sat at breakfast with Lucas while he'd talked for over an hour about Porter, Hannah, Tanner, and the rest of the Reese family, I'd finally learned a very valuable bit of information.

Lucas was gone forever.

It wrecked me to admit that, but it was the truth nonetheless.

Travis Reese went to sleep in my bed every night. He called me Charlotte, not Mom. He called Brady Brady, not Dad. He called my mom Susan and Tom Tom.

He could rattle off a million stories about his little sister, Hannah, but he refused to even hold Brady's son, William.

He was smart and funny and kind and witty.

And brave. Jesus, he was brave.

He loved ketchup but hated mustard (my favorite). And he loved pizza but hated pasta (Brady's favorite.) But, most surprising of all, when asked what his favorite food was, he waxed poetic about the sautéed mushrooms at The Porterhouse.

Yes. A ten-year-old's favorite food was his uncle's sautéed mushrooms.

I'd had those mushrooms when I'd stolen them off Porter's plate on our first date. Travis wasn't wrong. They were really freaking good. But I knew they had been better because I'd eaten them with Porter.

And, when I remembered my son picking the mushrooms out of the chicken tetrazzini I'd made one night, I knew that Porter was the reason Travis loved them as well.

Travis had been seeing a therapist every day, and it seemed like that was helping, but I knew he was struggling. He never cried, publicly anyway. I did though. A lot. To the point where it felt like I was drowning in tears. I was so overwhelmed that I couldn't breathe. Having a son I didn't know was hard. So hard that I'd inadvertently turned the reins over to someone who I'd hoped knew what they were doing.

Brady and Tom had been running the show since the day Lucas had been kidnapped, and that had not changed when Travis had been found. For the last week, I'd sat back and done my best to keep the drama to a minimum. But nothing had changed. And, judging by Brady's shit fit that had nearly landed him in a jail cell for the night, it was never going to change.

"Are you going to talk to me?" Brady asked as he put the car into park in front of my apartment and cut the ignition.

I didn't reply as I got out, heading straight for my front door.

"Charlotte," he called.

But I was in no mood for any more of his shit.

Or anyone's, for that matter.

"How'd it go?" Mom asked nervously as I marched inside, Brady right behind me.

The door wasn't even shut before I started shimmying, fighting against the pastel straitjacket until I got it over my head, leaving me in a cream camisole and a black pencil skirt. "This shirt is hideous," I declared, stomping to the trashcan and slinging it inside. "Let me do my own damn shopping from now on."

"Uh…" Mom drawled.

Brady stopped in the entryway and planted his hands on his hips. "New hearing in two weeks. The order of protection remained in place."

"Thank God," Tom grumbled, pulling my mom into a side hug.

"Charlotte!" Travis yelled, barreling out of the bedroom as fast as his skinny legs could carry him. "What happened?

When can I go home?"

"Hey, bud," Brady cooed.

Travis flicked his gaze to his father then right back to me. "Is Dad coming to get me?"

My heart shattered at the excitement dancing in his eyes.

Swallowing hard, I shuffled to him. "I'm sorry, baby. The judge rescheduled another hearing for two weeks from now."

Tilting his head back, he blinked those big, brown doe eyes up at me. "W…why?"

His staggering disappointment stole my breath. "I…um."

What the hell was I supposed to tell him? We'd tried to be honest with him since the get-go, but he was just a kid. He couldn't possibly understand the inner workings of this kind of hell. Truth be told, I didn't understand them, either. This whole thing was a clusterfuck of epic proportions.

"Because the judge thinks it's best if you stay with us," Brady replied when words failed me.

"Forever?" Travis croaked, training his pleading gaze on me.

I caught his hand and gave it a squeeze. "At least for two more weeks."

"But hopefully forever," Brady added. "You belong with us."

I bulged my eyes at him over my shoulder in a silent, *Shut the fuck up*, and when I turned back, Travis's lip was quivering.

"But I want my dad," he whispered, barely holding tears back.

I gave his hand another squeeze that was as much for me as it was for him. "I know. And I promise it's going to be okay. The judge just wants a little while longer to figure all this out."

His shoulders shook as his breathing shuddered, not a tear falling from his eyes but sobs ravaging him all the same.

Releasing his hand, I tried to gather him into a hug, but he struggled against me.

"Let me go!"

"Travis. Baby," I whispered, desperate to erase his pain.

He tore out of my arms and dashed to the bedroom before slamming the door behind him.

"Shit," I breathed, my shoulders sagging.

"He'll be okay," my mom soothed, but her voice was too thick for me to believe she was telling the truth.

"It's better this way," Brady said, resting his hand on my back.

Swear to God—it burned.

"How is it better this way?" I snapped, spinning to face him. "He's hurting!"

"He needs to understand that—"

"He's ten!" I spat, careful to keep my voice low. "Wasn't that your big argument today at the courthouse when Porter suggested he get a say in where he should live?"

He twisted his lips. "Yeah. But—"

"But nothing! He doesn't understand. And he's *never* going to understand why you kept him away from a good and decent man."

His face turned hard. "Don't start this shit, Charlotte. You got played. You have no fucking idea who Porter Reese really is."

"Neither do you!" I hissed. "But I can guarantee you our little boy does."

"Charlotte," Tom called.

"Get out!" I snarled. Stepping away from Brady, I sliced my gaze through the room. "*All* of you!"

Brady looked surprised.

Tom looked hurt.

And I steeled myself for Mom's reaction. Only, when my eyes made it to her, she appeared downright proud.

"All right, boys. You heard her. Let's get going." She herded the guys to the door.

"And tomorrow? *Call* before showing up," I added. "Brady, I'll bring him over to your place for dinner tomorrow night. But we need to talk."

As he made his way to the door, he stared at me, his jaw ticking with what was surely a few choice words he was struggling to keep in, but I couldn't have cared less. He could say whatever the hell he wanted or even waggle his magical finger of blame at me.

I was done with the bullshit.

It was time for a change, and it was starting with me.

After a few icy goodbyes, I shut and locked the front door.

Kicking off my shoes, I made my way down the hall.

"Travis?" I called softly, knocking on the bedroom door.

"Go away," he replied, tears evident in his voice.

I rested my forehead on the door. "They all left. It's just me and you now. You want some dinner?"

"I wanna go home!"

"I know. But it's only two more weeks and then I promise I'll talk to the judge myself."

"Go…away!" he yelled on a wheeze.

My lips thinned. See, this was exactly the problem with getting him worked up over Porter. At the end of the day, he was sick and this kind of emotional upheaval took a toll on his already frail body. This was stressful for us all, but for him, it was life-threatening.

I tested the doorknob, finding it locked. "Can I at least come in and listen to your lungs?"

"No!" he shouted before breaking into a fit of coughing.

"Listen, I'm going to set up your nebulizer. I'll give you a few minutes, but then you *have* to come out. Okay?"

When he didn't scream at me again, I went to the bathroom to set up his breathing treatment.

Going through the motions, I set his nebulizer up, slightly tweaking his medication to counteract the emotional damage caused by this afternoon. Thankfully, he had an appointment with his cardiologist in the morning. That would at least put my mind at ease about his heart after the last few days, but I needed to talk to Brady about maybe not laying everything out to Travis until we had firm answers. There was no reason for him to be this upset all the time.

"All right. I'm ready!" I called down the hall.

No reply.

"Travis?" I said, knocking on the door. "Baby, it's time."

No reply.

I pressed my ear to the door, listening for any kind of movement, only to be greeted by the most deafening sound of my life.

No coughing.

No wheezing.

No crying.

Nothing but bone-chilling silence.

Chills broke out across my skin, my body igniting in a

wildfire while the blood drained from my face.

"Travis!" I screamed, pounding on the locked door, fear prickling at my scalp.

No reply.

My heart thundered, and I frantically tried to twist the knob while pressing my shoulder against the wood to no avail.

"Oh God. Oh God. Oh God," I chanted as I raced to the bathroom. With jerky movements, I snatched the linen closet open, dumped my entire box of makeup onto the floor, and searched through the wreckage until I found a lone bobby pin.

After racing back to the door, I shoved it into the small hole on the lock. My hands were shaking so badly I had to try several times before it caught, visions of my son's lifeless body flashing on my lids with every blink.

Finally, I twisted the knob and slung the door open.

The room was empty.

Just like my chest.

"Travis!" My mind fired in a million different directions as I began scouring my bedroom.

I went straight to the ensuite bathroom. Empty.

I snatched the covers off the bed. Empty.

I tore through the closet. Empty.

And then the past roared to life, swallowing me whole. The darkness washed over me, darker than ever before.

He was gone.

Again.

"Lucas!" I screamed at the top of my lungs, panic consuming me.

Racing to the window, I found it open, but he was nowhere in sight.

On shaky legs, I climbed out the window, landing in the mulch-filled flowerbed before taking off at a dead sprint.

"Lucas!" I yelled, my voice echoing off the surrounding apartments. When he still didn't answer, I raced around the building, praying with my every turn that he would be there.

Panting, I scanned the parking lot, desperate for just one glimpse of his dark hair, hope fading into agony with every passing second.

Oh God. This was not happening.

"Lucas!" I choked out, spinning in a tight circle.

I was on the verge of hyperventilating when movement in the bushes caught my attention.

"Lucas!" I shrieked with relief when I saw his tear-soaked face peering at me through the leaves.

He was crouched, doing his best to hide, but his legs were too long to get him low enough to fully disappear.

My heart exploded and the ground swayed beneath my feet, but nothing could have stopped me from getting to him.

Branches cut and scraped my legs as I waded into them after him. "Oh God, Lucas."

He batted my hand away. "I'm not Lucas!"

Tears finally hit my eyes, my fear transforming into anger. "What the hell are you doing?" I cried.

"I'm going home!" he yelled before doubling over with heaving breaths.

Using his arm, I guided him out of the bushes, but he fought me every step of the way. "Christ, Travis. I thought I'd lost you again."

His nostrils flared, and his lips trembled. "You're never going to let me see him again, are you?"

"It's not my decision."

"Why not?" He gasped for air. "Why can't it be your decision? You're supposedly my mom, right?"

"No supposedly about it. I *am* your mom, and Brady *is* your dad."

"No, he's not! I hate him."

"No, you don't," I whispered.

He balled his fists at his sides and planted his weight on one foot as he leaned toward me and screamed, "Yes, I do! I hate all of you!"

I blanched, rocking back on a heel. He was a kid. A scared, confused, angry kid.

But that still seared through me like a scorching hot knife to the chest.

I didn't let it show. "I know this is hard, but we love you."

"You don't love me!" His face crumbled, and his shoulders shook violently. "You love *Lucas*. And my mom, she just wanted me to replace her dead son, Travis. But my dad—my *real* dad—he's the only one who ever wanted *me!*" He collapsed to his knees in the grass before falling forward to his hands, sucking in sharp, heaving breaths.

I followed him down, rubbing his back, because quite honestly, I had no idea what else to do.

Every word he'd said had cut me like the rusty, jagged blade of reality.

Because, as much as I wanted to deny it...

He wasn't wrong.

NINE

Porter

"**H**ERE, YOU BE KEN," HANNAH OFFERED, HOLDING OUT A naked male doll who thankfully had a pair of tighty-whities painted on. She'd been desperately trying to change the subject since the conversation had started.

I couldn't blame her. I wanted to change it too.

Today hadn't gone well at the courthouse. And, while staring down the barrel of at least two weeks before we even had the possibility of seeing Travis again, I had to tell her something.

Her questions weren't going to stop, but honestly, I didn't have many answers. So I told her the facts. Travis wasn't staying with a friend—he was staying with his birth parents. Why I'd thought her naïve mind could understand that when I could barely comprehend the madness of it all, I had no idea.

Her first question had been if Travis was in heaven with their mom. With that, a whole new pain had taken up residence inside me. But I'd been forced to finish the conversation.

I took the doll from her and set it aside. "Do you understand what I'm saying, Hannie?" I asked, my voice rough like sandpaper.

I was lying flat on my back in the middle of her bedroom floor, a discarded tea party on my left, a Barbie dream house on my right, my daughter straddling my stomach as she sat on top of me.

Thanks to my mom, her long, unruly, brown hair had been braided to look like her favorite princess, and she toyed with the end of it over her shoulder. Her chocolate-brown eyes, which matched her mother's, lifted to mine. "Does he still love us?"

I'd changed out of my suit the minute we'd gotten home and pulled on a pair of jeans and a T-shirt that was going to have to be burned after this conversation. There was no way I'd ever be able to wear it again with the memories of her devastation clinging to it.

"Of course," I assured her, sitting up and wrapping her in a hug. "He's always going to love us. And we're always going to love him."

"Do I have to get a new mommy and daddy too?"

An ache filled my hollow chest. "No. Never," I swore. "I'm your only daddy. And your mom was your only mommy."

"So, why does Travis have two?"

I sighed, kicking myself in the ass for not asking my mom to be a part of this discussion. "Well..." I started only to trail off when my phone rang in my pocket.

And, much like her offer for me to play Ken, I, too, was suddenly desperate for a way out of not only this conversation, but this situation as well.

"Hold that thought," I said, digging into my back pocket.

I lifted the screen into my line of sight, and then all at once, the oxygen was sucked from the room. Shifting her to one side, I burst up off the floor with her still in my arms.

One word flashing on my phone sent an avalanche of adrenaline crashing down on me.

"Charlotte?" I said, pressing my phone to my ear.

"Come over," she pleaded in a hushed and urgent tone.

"What's wrong?" I asked, dashing from the room to collect my keys and wallet.

"Everything," she cried. "God, Porter. *Everything.*"

My heart lurched, and fear iced my veins. "What's going on? Talk to me. Is Travis okay?"

"He's fine," she choked out through tears. "He's doing a breathing treatment. Please, just come over. Come over. Come over."

Relief only washed the fear away—the anxiety was permanent.

Hannah held tight to my neck as I jogged through our house, pausing only to slip a pair of shoes on before I was out the door.

"I'm on my way. Stay on the phone."

"I have to go. He's almost finished."

I planted Hannah in her car seat, buckled her in, and then hurried around to the driver's side. "Charlotte, wait." With a flick of the key, my Tahoe roared to life, and I snatched it into gear.

"I have to go," she breathed.

A plethora of words danced on the tip of my tongue.

Everything ranging from, *Are you okay?* to *I love you.* But, as I flew out of my neighborhood, one destination in mind, "I'll be there soon," were the only ones that escaped.

It took me thirty agonizing minutes to get to her apartment. Hannah asked approximately seven thousand questions on the way over. I answered exactly none of them. I debated on swinging past my parents' house to drop her off, but that might have been our only chance to see Travis, and damn it, I wasn't taking that away from either of them.

During the drive, my head swirled.

Hope was telling me she was going to give him back.

Fear was telling me she was setting me up to break the protection order.

My mind was telling me she was hurting and scared.

My soul was telling me she was hurting and needed me.

But, through it all, my son's dark-brown eyes and wide smile guided my path.

"Where are we?" Hannah asked as I unbuckled her from her car seat.

I blew out a ragged breath and stared at the sidewalk that led to Charlotte's front door—to him. "Travis's new house."

Nerves rolled in my stomach, and my heart was beating so hard I thought it might burst from my chest, but she gasped so loudly I couldn't help but smile.

"Can I see him?" she breathed in excitement.

"God, I hope so," I admitted.

One foot in front of the other, my legs devoured the distance to her door.

I knocked once, blew out an anxious sigh, and then knocked again.

My hand was still poised in the air when she swung it open.

"Hi," she squeaked. Her face was pale, and her hollow eyes were red-rimmed, dark circles supporting them from the bottom. She looked a lot like the woman lost in the darkness that I'd first met at that spring fling. And it fucking killed to see her like that, knowing the breathtaking smiles and heart-stopping laughs she was capable of.

I forced a grin. "Hi."

Her gaze flicked to Hannah, who was on my hip, and she shot me a tight smile that made her chin quiver. "He's in the bedroom."

Reaching out, I caught the back of her neck and pulled her against me.

She came willingly, her hand going to my free hip and twisting into my T-shirt.

"Are you okay?" I asked before pressing my lips to her forehead.

"No," she croaked. "But *he* will be." She stepped out of my reach and swung a hand toward the bedroom. "Go. We can talk later."

She didn't have to tell me twice. With hurried steps, I carried Hannah straight to Charlotte's bedroom. Not even bothering with a knock, I shoved the door open wide.

And then the most indescribable peace I had ever experienced washed over me as my world finally stilled.

Travis's head snapped up from the iPad he'd been playing on. He didn't look any different than the last time I'd seen him.

He was too thin.

Too pale.

Too sick.

But, when I saw him now, he did look a lot like Charlotte. And he was still one hundred percent mine.

"Dad!" he screamed, exploding off the bed.

I raced toward him, not stopping until he collided with my front.

"Dad," he repeated, wrapping his arms around my waist, his shoulders shaking in time with my own.

"Hey, Trav," I choked out, patting his back while setting my squirming daughter down so she could get in on the love too.

"Travis!" she giggled, stepping into his side, mirroring his hold on me, and hugging the life out of him.

Warmth filled my chest as I dropped to my knees and palmed each side of his face. I planted a kiss to his forehead that, only a week ago, he would have complained about. Now, he wiggled even closer, tears streaming down his cheeks.

I sat at the foot of the bed, and he followed me closely, wedging himself between my legs, Hannah still attached to him.

He rested his head against my shoulder like he had done so often when he had been younger, but not in years.

"How you doing, buddy?" I asked quietly, smoothing his hair down before pressing another kiss to the top of his head.

"I want to come home," he whined.

"I know. I want that too."

He peered up at me expectantly. "Then why can't I?"

The vise on my chest wrenched tight, and I lifted my gaze to the doorway.

Charlotte was standing there, twin rivers pouring from her eyes, a myriad of emotions etched in her face, all of them terrorizing her.

With my heart in my throat, I glanced around at the absolute devastation Catherine had caused all of us.

My son was fighting the battle of his life with his health; he didn't need this shit on top of it.

My daughter was hurting and confused because she was losing her big brother and best friend.

Charlotte had been lost for almost a decade, and now, she had her son back, but she was living, breathing, and suffering through his pain the way any good mother would.

And I... Well, I was falling apart. But I was also the only one left to pick up the pieces.

"We're going to figure this out," I announced to the entire room. "I'm here now. And we're together. That's all that matters."

Charlotte nodded and started to back out of the room.

"Sweetheart," I called, and her sad gaze lifted to mine. "Thank you," I whispered.

She nodded again and started to pull the door closed.

My body screamed for me to stop her.

To ask her to stay.

To drag her into the darkness and ease both of our hearts.

But, judging by Travis's death grip around my neck, my son needed some time with his father in the light.

"Don't go far," I told her.

She slid her gaze to Travis. "I couldn't if I tried."

"Charlotte," I breathed in apology.

She faked a smile. "I'll see what I can drum up for dinner." She paused and then added, "For all of us."

The door clicked softly behind her.

My body sagged in a confusing mixture of relief and defeat.

"Daddy," Hannah whispered, patting my thigh.

I looked down at her. "Yeah?"

With wide eyes, she shook her head. "Guess what? There's no TV in Travis's new room."

"There's no TV in the whole place," Travis complained.

I slapped a hand over my heart and cried out dramatically, "Oh God, say it ain't so!"

Travis glowered.

Hannah giggled.

And I smiled because, regardless that our lives were in shambles, in that moment, with Travis on my right and Hannah on my left, everything was right.

Over the next two hours, the three of us stayed locked in that room. Alone while the chaos of reality continued to roar outside.

Travis asked questions I didn't have the answers to. I made promises I couldn't possibly uphold. But, for those minutes with him lying in the bed beside me, a game of Minecraft playing on his iPad, his heart beating slow and steady, his breaths even and easy, I felt not an ounce of guilt for lying to him.

He needed that.

The simple.

The predictable.

The monotony.

And, a few hours later, as he fell asleep next to his sister, the sun barely sinking over the horizon, I learned how badly they both needed it.

And I had a feeling they weren't the only ones.

TEN

Charlotte

WAS SITTING ON MY COUCH, MY KNEES PULLED TO MY CHEST, a glass of untouched wine on the end table, my mind lost in thought, when I heard the bedroom door open.

I fought the urge to fly up off the couch.

"Pizza's on the counter," I called, keeping my eyes aimed at the wall. "I wasn't sure what kind you guys would like so I got a few different—ooph."

I was cut off when Porter's hard body hit me. One of his arms hooked under my knees, the other wrapping around my back. And then the couch disappeared from beneath me.

"What the—"

"Shh!" he demanded.

"What are you doing?" I whisper-yelled, looping my arms around his neck to balance myself.

"Your apartment's too small," he rumbled, carrying me straight to the bathroom in the hallway.

"I'm working on getting a house. It's just taking some time."

"Mm," he hummed, setting my ass on the bathroom vanity. Bending at the waist, he rested his hands on either side of me and got in my face, his piercing, blue eyes searching mine. "Please tell me you believe me when I say that I had nothing to do with Catherine taking your son."

"I…uh…know. I heard your message."

His gaze darkened. "You listen to all of it?"

I licked my lips and nodded. "I just got it last night. Brady blocked your number on my phone."

"Right," he mumbled.

"I'm sorr—"

"I had no fucking idea he was your son. You have to believe me or this is as far as we can ever go."

My heart swelled. "I believe you."

He eyed me warily and then warned, "No faking it, Charlotte."

I leaned into him and brushed my lips with his. "I believe you, Porter."

In one swift movement, he locked the bathroom door and flipped the lights off.

I gasped as the familiar darkness flooded the room. My whole body sagged, but my pulse quickened in anticipation.

Porter's large frame moved toward me, his hips forcing my knees apart as he wedged his body between them. Gliding a hand into the back of my hair, he tucked my face into his neck. "Talk to me."

"I don't know what to say," I lied, fisting the back of his shirt and nuzzling my cheek against his jaw, the most amazing calm of my life engulfing me.

Using my hair to turn my head, he swept his lips up my neck, and then his breath flittered across my skin as he whispered in my ear, "No questions. No judgments. No faking it. No apologies. Give it to me."

A shiver traveled down my spine, and I swayed into him, our chests becoming flush.

And then I gave it to him. Everything I could never give anyone else.

"I think he hates me."

No sooner than the words had cleared my lips, he followed it up with a confession of his own. "I'm drowning in that car all over again without him."

My breath hitched, an apology burning on the tip of my tongue. But that wasn't what Porter and I did in the darkness.

Turning my head, I brushed my lips with his. "He told me that I only loved Lucas, and Catherine only wanted him to replace Travis." I paused to collect myself. "He thinks you were the only one who ever wanted him."

His body turned to stone, but his head hung low. "Jesus."

My throat became thick, and I was barely able to speak. "I love him. I swear I do. But he's right. I want him to be Lucas."

His fingers tensed in my hair, but the pain at my scalp did nothing to distract me from the anguish in my chest.

"God, it feels so filthy even saying it out loud. You have to know that I love him. Down to the core of my soul, but he's like a stranger to me." I tried to push off the counter, desperate for some space, but Porter moved in closer, blocking my retreat.

"He *was* a stranger to me once. Now, he *is* the core to

my soul. He and Hannah. That's my life. That love wasn't ingrained into me at birth the way it was you, but it grew into a wildfire. And I don't know how to turn it off. And I'm terrified the courts are going to ask me to do just that."

"Oh God," I breathed, hooking my legs around his hips and locking them at the ankle as if I could hug him tight enough to erase the pain.

His hand drifted down my back and then crept under the hem of my shirt, flesh to flesh. "Your turn, Charlotte."

"I can't give him to you."

"I'll never ask you to. But I won't ever stop trying to get him back."

My body locked up tight, panic blasting through my system. "W...what?"

He shook his head and pressed his lips to my temple. "There's enough of him for both of us. It doesn't have to be one or the other. He's your son. But I'm begging you not to forget that he's mine too."

Closing my eyes, even though the room was already pitch-black, I whispered, "I have no idea what I'm doing. These should be the happiest days of my life, and I can't stop crying because I know he's hurting."

His head came up, and while I couldn't see him, I could feel his blue stare burning into me. "You're hurting too."

It wasn't a question.

It wasn't an accusation.

It also wasn't a lie.

"We're all hurting," I admitted, clinging to his shoulders.

"Not tonight," he whispered. "Tonight, he's happy. Tonight, I'm here with you. Tonight, we're together. Tonight, nothing outside this apartment matters. Tonight, your son sleeps safely in your bed. Tonight, my kids sleep soundly for the first time in a week. And, tonight, we can share the darkness."

My mind drifted back to only a few weeks earlier, the first time Porter had taken me to the confessional in the darkness. It was a night I'd never forget because it was the first time I'd ever given myself to someone else. Not physically, though that had happened too. But emotionally. I'd offered him my deepest, darkest secrets. And he'd taken them, devoured them, and made them his own. He'd made the darkness a beautiful place filled with understanding and acceptance.

Porter was like that. Everything was easier with him

Everything except losing him.

So I asked him the same question he'd asked me that first night together. "What's going to happen when we turn on the lights?"

"Just don't let go and it won't matter."

"How are we going to do this? Technically, Porter, you're breaking the law by even being here. The police—"

"I had *nothing* to do with the kidnapping," he growled.

"I know! And I believe you. But the police are still investigating you. You end up in jail for breaking the protection order, it's not going to help anyone."

"So we lay low for a few weeks. But, damn it, Charlotte, we will find a way to make this work. This is my life. This is *your* life. This is *his* life. And *her* life. This is *our* life and you know it. We'll figure out the details later, but for now, all I need from you is a promise that we are going to do this. No matter what. We're in this together."

My heart soared higher than I ever thought possible.

Porter had the most amazing knack of getting into my sub-
conscious and untying the knots I so often made out of ob-
stacles. With him, my thoughts weren't jumbled and my fears
weren't roadblocks.

"God, I missed you," I breathed, giving him my very last
confession.

"Does that mean you're with me?"

"Yeah, baby. I'm with you."

"And we're going to do this, right?"

"Yeah. We're going to do this."

And then Porter gave me his last confession, only his was
a little more tangible.

His lips crashed down on mine, our mouths opening and
our tongues tangling, needy and desperate.

His lips felt like velvet, smooth even as they were rough
and demanding. And, with his every touch, a week's worth of
panic and anxiety ebbed from my system. In its absence, every
nerve ending in my body came alive, desire filling me.

I tugged at the bottom of his shirt, frantic to feel more of
him—all of him.

He broke the kiss long enough to snatch it over his head,
mine meeting the same fate less than a second later.

His mouth once again covered mine, and he yanked my
bra down, both of my breasts popping free of the cups. His
dexterous fingers immediately found my nipples, plucking
and rolling, sending sparks to my clit.

"Yes," I breathed, falling back on the sink until my shoulders hit the cold mirror.

Using my legs to force him forward, I rolled my hips
against his, finding glorious friction against his hard length

hidden behind his zipper.

"Fuck," he ground out, releasing my breasts and moving his hands down to my core. His fingers dipped into my yoga pants, swept my panties to the side, and then pressed in deep.

My back arched and my ass slipped off the vanity, but Porter held me in place with an arm hooked under my hips.

"Keep going," he encouraged in a jagged voice as I began working myself against his hand. His thumb dropped to my clit, drawing slow circles as his fingers curled inside me. "Come on, sweetheart. Give it to me," he urged before hunching over to suck my nipple into his mouth.

The combination was too much, beautiful and agonizing at the same time. My nerve endings became overloaded with sensations to the point I couldn't focus anymore, but Porter never slowed.

His fingers twisted.

His tongue swirled.

His thumb circled.

"Porter," I cried, my release tearing through me.

His head popped up, sealing over my mouth as he swallowed my moans until I sagged in his arms.

And then…he was gone.

My pants were ripped down my legs, and the sound of his zipper played the harmony to my labored breathing.

And then…he was *everywhere*.

His mouth came back to mine, his hand guided his thick shaft to my entrance, and his strong body surged forward as he drove inside me.

I clung to his shoulders as he dragged me to the edge of the counter, the lip of it biting into my ass as his hips began a relentless rhythm that lit the fuse on yet another orgasm.

"Oh God," I moaned as he planted himself at the hilt.

"Shh," he ordered, pressing up onto his toes to change the angle, as if he could possibly get deeper. "You have to be quiet."

I nodded even though he couldn't see me, yet he somehow understood.

He resumed his tortuous rhythm, driving into me in the hunt for his own release. "Fuck, Charlotte," he groaned, his breaths coming quicker, his shaft swelling inside me.

He was close.

I was closer.

Circling my hips, I ground against him. "Baby," I called in a whisper.

"I'm right here, Charlotte," he swore. "Always."

My release climbed higher until I wasn't sure I could hold on any longer, and when I felt Porter step off the edge, I eagerly followed him over.

He folded forward, burying his face in my neck, his hips never faltering as we rode our orgasms out together.

Lazily, I trailed my fingertips up and down his back, his large frame hovering over me, both of us panting.

"Jesus," he breathed.

I smiled.

Righting himself, he gripped my hips so I didn't teeter off the edge of the counter and grumbled, "Why is there never a fucking bed in the darkness?"

There was no way I could have stopped the loud bubble of laughter that came from my throat.

His shoulders shook as he joined me. Cupping the back of my neck, he pressed his smiling lips to mine in a kiss that meant more to me than he would ever be able to comprehend. Sans the incredible sex that had preceded it, there was nothing special about that kiss.

But maybe that was what made it so perfect.

It was easy, and it made the overwhelming world outside my apartment feel easy too.

"Close your eyes. I'm gonna turn on the lights," he whispered.

My stomach sank, and I gripped his shoulders tight. "Nothing's going to change when you do, right?"

He caught my hand and folded his around it, intertwining our fingers before bringing it to his lips. "Everything's going to change, Charlotte. And I swear to you, no matter what happens, we're going to do that together, okay?"

My nose began to sting. Fucking Porter and his hand holding.

God, I loved it so much.

"Okay, baby. Turn on the lights."

"I didn't know!" I defended.

Porter smirked across the kitchen, his hip propped against the counter and his long legs crossed at the ankle. "Seven?"

"I didn't know!" I repeated.

After we'd cleaned up, which was surprisingly convenient when you have sex in the bathroom, we'd gotten dressed and begrudgingly left our private sanctuary. I hadn't been eating much over the last few days, and with Porter securely holding my hand, making my mind blessedly quiet, food had become a priority. On the way to the kitchen, I'd stopped at the bedroom door, cracking it open to peer in at Travis, as I had done so many times over the last few days. Every time I'd done it before, half of me had expected him not to be there. That fear had become a reality only hours earlier, after he'd climbed out the window in an attempt to escape me.

But that escape had become the precipice that had brought Porter back to us.

"Seven though?" he teased, lifting a piece of pizza to his mouth.

I glared at him, all the while smiling on the inside. "Well, he likes mushrooms." I waved my hand at one box before amending, "Sometimes, anyway." I swung my hand toward another box. "But then I wasn't sure about Hannah, but all kids like cheese, right?"

He swallowed a bite and washed it down with beer before saying, "So that's two. You got five more to go."

I took a sip of my wine. Not the warm one from the end table. Porter had poured me a new glass. "Well, I figured, with you being a grown man, you'd probably want yours to be a little heartier. I'm sorry to say they didn't have your precious Wagyu on the menu, but I got you all the other meats."

He smiled wide and counted off, "Three," before taking another bite.

"Seriously, Porter?" I huffed, not even the least bit annoyed. "Fine. I like supreme, but I remembered you picking the onions out of your salad that night at The Porterhouse, so I got one with onions and one without in case you wanted a piece of mine."

He lifted three fingers in the air and, one by one, flipped up two more to show five. "For the record, I like onions, but you didn't order onions that night, and I had high hopes of my mouth being on yours by the end of the evening, so I made the sacrifice in the name of onion breath." He winked. "Two more."

My stomach got all warm and fluttery at the thought of our first kinda-sorta kiss. He'd only brushed his lips with mine, and even before I had known how perfect his mouth truly was, I still would have killed for more. He could have eaten a field of onions and I wouldn't have cared.

Rolling my eyes, I finished with, "Then I thought maybe Travis wouldn't like mushrooms, so I got sausage. Everyone likes sausage. Except...then I thought maybe it was ground beef that everyone liked." I shrugged. "So I ordered both. There. Are you happy now?"

He set the rest of his crust aside and prowled over to me. "Happy to be standing here, surrounded by seven pizzas that had to have cost you at least a hundred bucks and are now more than likely going to go to waste? No." His hand came up to my face, his thumb trailing back and forth across my cheek. "Happy to be standing here, listening to you pretend to be annoyed with me while rambling on about ordering at least a hundred bucks in pizza because you weren't sure what kind we would like, but you knew I needed that time alone with Travis as much as he needed it with me, and you didn't want to interrupt to ask what kind of toppings we liked on our pizza and, instead, just ordered the left side of the menu? Yeah. Charlotte. I'm really fucking happy."

I bit my bottom lip. "It was only seventy dollars. I had a coupon."

A wide, breathtaking smile split his face. "Beautiful *and*

thrifty. I knew I was falling in love with you for a reason."

"Porter," I whispered, my whole body warming. "Don't say you love me."

His hands went to my hips where he tugged me against him. "I didn't say I love you. I said I was *falling* in love with you. And it has nothing to do with pizza and everything to do with the fact that you called me tonight."

"He needed you."

"*You* needed me too, Charlotte. And believe me, that is *not* something I take lightly. Because I really fucking needed you too. You are the strongest woman I have ever met. You've lived through hell, and I know you think you were barely surviving, and maybe some days you were, but you kept holding on when others would have let go. You never needed me to stop the world for you. You simply needed someone to accept you for who you were. But, tonight, after a week that's shaved years off my life and left me questioning everything I've ever known, you stopped it for me. And you stopped it for Travis too. I don't know what's going to happen when the sun comes up tomorrow. And I don't know what the judge is going to say in two weeks. But because of you, I have tonight. So yeah, Charlotte. My last confession of the night is that I've been falling in love with you since the first day I met you." He settled his hands on either side of my face and bent at the knees so we were eye to eye. "And, sweetheart, you have to know that, with a woman like you, it's a really short trip."

"Don't say that," I pleaded, but my heart was swelling.

He tipped his forehead down until it was resting on mine. "We can pretend if you want. But it's still true."

"We still have a long way to go, Porter. Don't complicate

this any more than it already is."

Smirking, he asked, "Sweetheart, our road has never been smooth. Not for a single second since you brought me that fucking pickle jar at the spring fling. And yet you think me loving you is going to change when the road gets bumpy?"

"It could."

"It won't."

"But it could, and I think the two of us have suffered enough heartbreak to last a lifetime. Don't add this to the list."

"Charlotte, your name had been carved on the top of that list for over a month." He sucked in a deep breath, released me, and strolled back over to the counter, where he resumed his position. Lifting a piece of supreme pizza (with onions) out of the box, he smiled. "But, if this is what you need, I'll give it to you. Just let me know when you're done pretending."

"I'm not pretending," I lied. I absolutely was. It was what I did best.

I wasn't ready to absorb what he was saying. Okay, that wasn't true. I wasn't ready to set myself up for disappointment again. All good things came to an end eventually. Even love. Not that I knew. The only person I'd ever truly loved had gone missing for ten years and now hated me.

"It's just—"

"Pepperoni," he interrupted, waving a slice of pizza in my direction.

"What?"

"One pepperoni and one whatever the hell you want. I'll eat either. Hannah likes cheese, but Travis likes pepperoni, so I pick them off for her when she isn't looking and voila: instant cheese pizza. *That's* what you order in the future."

I swallowed hard, unsure whether to accept the out he'd just offered me by changing the subject. But the fact that he was offering me the out meant everything.

So much so that I smiled at him and said, "I'm falling in love with you too. But, with a man like you, it's a *very long* trip. I'm still not completely convinced you aren't a serial killer."

Porter smiled. "You're such a liar."

"I speak nothing but the truth."

He cocked his head to the side, a mischievous glint shining in his eyes. "Oh yeah? *Nothing* but the truth?"

I made a show of crossing my heart.

"Okay, then. How many times have you listened to my voicemail?"

Oh shit. "Your voicemail?" I played stupid and got busy packing up the smorgasbord of leftover pizzas.

"You know, the one when I told you I loved you, like, a week ago. The one you confessed to only getting last night." His arrogant smile stretched wider. "The one you are now pretending you don't know about. And the one, I have no doubt, you listened to at least two dozen times because you love me too. And you missed me, most especially my sexy body."

I barked a laugh. "Wow. You are quite full of yourself tonight, aren't you?"

His heat hit my back, and his arms looped around my stomach. "No. I'm right."

"I listened to it once," I lied, resting my hands on top of his.

He chuckled and dipped low to press his lips to my neck.

My head lolled to the side to give him more room as he peppered kisses up to my ear.

"What happened to the truth?" he teased before nipping at my earlobe.

I purred, tracing my hand up his strong shoulders and into the back of his hair. "It got lost with your humility."

His chuckle turned into a full-blown laugh.

And then, as his hand slipped over my breast, mine turned into a full-blown moan.

Moments later, after a quick check to make sure the kids were still asleep, it turned into a full-blown repeat performance in the bathroom.

Only, this time, we left the lights on.

ELEVEN

Porter

"**H**ANNAH!" I HISSED. "LEAVE HER ALONE!"

My daughter turned to look at me, her face filled with awe as she stood over Charlotte. "She's still asleep."

"I know!" I hissed, waving an urgent hand to make her come back into the bedroom.

We'd been tiptoeing around her apartment all morning, trying to let her sleep. This included eating three bowls of cereal in her bed at six thirty in the morning, after Travis had woken up for a breathing treatment. Charlotte hadn't even budged as I'd crawled out from under her on the couch and headed down the hall to help my son. The hum of the nebulizer was loud, but we did our best to keep it quiet by going into the bathroom in Charlotte's bedroom and shutting both of the doors. I supposed she hadn't been sleeping any better than I had over the last week, and pair that with a night of awkward yet completely incredible sex in a cramped bathroom and I

111

figured she was down for the count.

It made me an epic weirdo, but I could have watched her peacefully sleeping for hours.

And it seemed my daughter shared the infatuation.

"Get over here!" I whisper-yelled, silently snapping my finger and pointing to the floor beside me.

Smiling, she skipped over and took my hand.

Shaking my head, I guided her back into the bedroom and quietly closed the door behind us.

"Travis, your new mommy sleeps a lot," she said, heading straight for the bed, where she climbed up to sit with her brother.

He didn't even look up from his iPad as he replied, "She's not my new mommy."

"Yeah. She is, Trav," I corrected.

His head never moved, but his eyes lifted to mine. "I already had a mom. She died. I don't need two."

Hannah's eyes lit. "I'll take her! I never had a mommy."

My gut twisted. "Hannie, you did have a mom. She's in heaven now." Or more likely hell, but my lies knew no bounds when it came to my children.

I walked over to the bed and sat on the side. Hannah crawled into my lap, while Travis watched me out of the corner of his eye, pretending he wasn't. I had to smile. Maybe he was more like Charlotte than I'd thought.

"Put that down for a second," I told him, shifting Hannah to one of my legs.

"Fine," he huffed and begrudgingly obeyed.

"She is your mom. And she loves you very much. When I first met Charlotte, she missed you so much that she was still struggling, even ten years later. I know this is weird and it's hard to understand, but she loves you more than you can ever imagine."

"She won't even let me see you though."

"That's going to change, okay? It might take a little while before we get everything set up. But I promise you we're all working to make that change."

"Not that Brady guy!" he exclaimed. "He's an asshole."

Hannah gasped so loudly I had to bite back a laugh.

"Hey!" I snapped my fingers. "Watch your mouth."

I set Hannah on her feet, and she wandered away, flashing Travis a pair of wide you-are-in-so-much-trouble eyes.

He sheepishly looked away. "Brady's always saying that it's best that I don't talk to you anymore. And he's mean to Charlotte too. He told his wife the other day that Charlotte was too weak to be a mom."

My jaw turned to granite. Yeah, I'd hated Brady before. But my son was right: He was an asshole. But, now, he was talking shit about my woman…in front of my kid? Fuck that.

"Don't worry about Brady," I clipped before getting my anger in check. "Charlotte and I are going to work together to make sure you're taken care of. But I need you to drop the attitude, okay? She thinks you hate her."

His sad eyes lifted to mine. "I do hate her."

I shook my head. "No, buddy. You just don't love her yet. There's a big difference."

He stared up at me with haunted eyes and asked, "Do you love her?"

"Yes," I answered curtly. "But, before you read into that, I don't know what's going to happen between the two of us.

There's still a long road to the future."

"Does she love you?"

I grinned. "Well, Charlotte is currently pretending she doesn't love me." I shot him a pointed wink. "But come on. We both know she does. I mean…look at me. How could she not?"

He giggled, and it eased the ache in my chest.

"She showed me a picture of you kissing her while we were at the police station."

"Oh yeah?" I drawled, shock and pride settling inside me.

"She said that you would trust her to do what was right for me."

I hooked my arm around his shoulders and pulled him into my side. "I do. And proof that I was right is that, last night, when you truly needed me, she called and told me to come over." I kissed the top of his head. "Give her a chance, Travis. I promise you won't regret it. She's pretty amazing."

He nodded, but he didn't quite seem convinced. Instead of harping on him about it, though, I decided to change the subject.

"Okay…now, let's—"

"Daddy!" Hannah shrieked, terror sharp in her tone.

I lurched off the bed and rushed toward her voice. She came sprinting out of Charlotte's closet until her body got tangled in some of the hanging clothes, and before I could reach her, the whole rod came down on top of her.

She cried, kicking and screaming under the mess.

After digging her out of what had to be Charlotte's entire winter wardrobe, I scooped her up to sit on my hip. "Hey. It's okay. Everything's fine."

Suddenly, the bedroom door flung open and an honest-to-God zombie came stumbling in.

Her hair was in tangles and sticking out in all directions, and she fought a losing battle with her lids in an attempt to open her eyes in the bright light. "Travis!" she called, sleep muffling her voice.

"Right here." He laughed, swinging a humor-filled smile my way.

She clutched her chest. "Are you okay?"

He laughed louder. "I'm good. You...uh...slept late."

"Jesus, what time is it?" Her gaze slowly slid to me, and then her whole body jerked. "Shit. I forgot you were here."

"And good morning to you too, beautiful." Chuckling, I walked over and kissed her forehead. Using my free hand, I smoothed her hair down. "You look particularly stunning this morning. You sleep well?"

She curled into my side. "I don't even know what day it is."

"That's a good sign." I glanced up and found Travis watching us closely, his eyes aimed at her hand casually resting on my stomach.

And then, like a lightning bolt had struck her, she jerked again. "Oh my God. Did you go all night without a breathing treatment?"

"I took care of it," I announced.

"Oh." She peered up at me. "You should have woken me up. I tweaked his medication last—"

"I saw."

"Yeah, but..."

I squeezed her hip. "Seriously, Charlotte. For as

meticulously as you had everything laid out, Hannah could have administered it."

Travis laughed. "She so could have."

"Well, it's always better to be prepared. Things can get confusing in the middle of the night."

I smirked. "I know. I could barely concentrate over your snores from the couch."

Travis cackled and folded over on the bed.

"I don't snore!"

I gave her a teasing side-eye. "You sure about that?"

Swinging her head between Travis and me, she defended, "I don't!"

Travis decided to get in on the joke. "I don't know, Charlotte. That's not the way it sounded in here."

Her mouth fell open, but her smile showed around it. "Don't you dare side with him."

Travis kept the joke going for longer than it was funny, but judging by Charlotte's grin and my boy's howls of laughter, neither of them minded.

"Fine. I might have snored. But you keep rubbing it in and I won't be making pancakes for breakfast."

"Breakfast? It's, like, lunch!" He laughed.

She planted her hands on her hips in the most dramatic, non-Charlotte way possible and shot back, "Fine. You keep it up and I won't make pancakes for *lunch*."

I couldn't help but stare. She'd always been so dry and unreadable. But, right then, bantering with our son, she was downright playful. I guessed that was what she looked like when she was happy.

And Christ, she was beautiful.

I lifted a hand in Travis's direction to silence him. "Whoa. Okay, chill. Let's not get crazy. I'm going to need to eat more than a bowl of Cheerios today."

"Oh, I didn't say I was making any for you." She smiled, and then her eyes flashed wide as she leaned to the side to see around me. "Wow! What happened there?" She pointed at the mess in her closet.

"Sorry about that. Hannah got tangled in your clothes. I'll fix it…after pancakes."

Hannah's head snapped up off my shoulder, and she looked to Charlotte, whispering, "There's a man in your closet."

Charlotte waved her off. "Nah. That's just Ian. He's harmless."

I closed one eye, cupped a hand to my ear, and leaned toward her. "I'm sorry. Did you say *Ian*?"

"Yeah. Ian Somerhalder," she answered like it wasn't the most ludicrous thing I'd ever heard come out of her mouth.

"You have some guy named *Ian* in your closet?" I clarified, because really, what the hell else was there to say?

Upon stepping over the mountain of clothes, she dug into the back of her closet and pulled out a life-size cutout of some dude with his arms crossed, his steely-blue, cardboard, smoldering gaze staring out into oblivion.

"What. Is. That?" Travis asked, rising from the bed to inspect the absurdity.

She shrugged. "Apparently, he plays a vampire on some TV show. The residents at the hospital gave this guy to me for my birthday. They used to call me a vampire because I worked such long hours at night."

I stared in awe at a woman I was suddenly realizing I

didn't know at all. "And you kept him? In your closet, like a dirty little secret?"

She grinned up at him. "What can I say? He has pretty eyes."

I barked a laugh and set my wiggling daughter on her feet so she, too, could check our newest guest out. "You know who else has pretty eyes?" I hooked my thumb at my chest. "Me. Your boyfriend, remember?"

She cocked her head to the side. "Aren't you a little old to be using the term *boyfriend*?"

"Woman, you have a nearly six-foot cardboard cutout of a TV vampire in your closet. I'm not sure you are in any position to be discussing age-appropriate behavior right now."

She crossed her arms over her chest, but not even her glare could hide her humor. "Did you seriously just call me *woman*?"

I mirrored her posture. "Did you seriously just produce a flat man out of your closet?"

"Oh my God." She giggled. "Are you jealous? Of a piece of cardboard?"

"Pshh...no," I replied, twisting my lips and looking to Travis for backup.

He gave me none.

"He's totally jealous," he said, tipping his head back to look at Charlotte.

Hannah patted her on the leg. "Are you really a vampire?"

"No," I answered. "She's a poor woman with a very serious hoarding problem." I plucked the stupid cutout from her hands. "And we are going to help her with this by tossing Ian here to the curb."

"You are not!" Charlotte exclaimed, grabbing the man's feet.

"Oh, but I am," I whispered.

Tug-of-war ensued. And, while I wasn't jealous in the least, I was having so much fun watching her interact with the kids that I would have kept the charade up for the rest of my life.

There was a woman I'd never thought I'd be able to get into the same room with my kids and she was joining forces with them against me. I fucking loved it.

"Porter, stop!" She laughed as I started toward the door, Ian firmly in my grasp, her dragging behind us.

"He's going to the dumpster," I declared.

Travis held her hips to try to help, and Hannah grabbed her brother's hips to complete the chain of people I loved. (Well, minus Ian, of course.)

"I'm willing to negotiate for his safety!" Charlotte laughed.

I froze but kept my hold on Ian tight. Arching an eyebrow, I said, "I'm listening."

Smiling, she bent and whispered something in Travis's ear.

"I want to hear!" Hannah cried, bouncing on her toes.

Travis scrubbed his chin while staring off into space. "I like this plan," he said.

Partitioning her mouth off, Charlotte whispered what I assumed was the same thing in Hannah's ear.

Her whole face lit, her brown eyes dancing with what could only be described as pure joy.

"We are prepared to offer the addition of chocolate chips

to the pancakes in exchange for Ian's safe return," Charlotte said.

I gave the cardboard cutout a sharp tug. "No deal."

"Come on, Dad!" Travis whined.

Putting a hand up to quiet him, Charlotte sucked in a long breath through her nose. With the most beautiful blank face I'd ever seen, she asked, "What if we were willing to add sausage on the side?"

My children stared at me expectantly. Neither of them ate sausage, but they knew I did.

It was a completely ridiculous conversation, but it filled my hollow chest in unimaginable ways.

One week earlier, I'd had my son snatched away from me.

One week earlier, I'd lost all hope of ever having my family again.

One week earlier, I'd sat in a police station with my entire life unrecognizable

Yet one week later, I had everything I could ever want in one room, all staring at me, waiting for me to agree to chocolate chip pancakes and sausage.

My instincts told me to shut the door, lock it, and ride out the rest of my life in that room with them. The world outside was entirely too dark for lights that bright.

I stared at Charlotte, flanked by my kids—her son—her smile wide, her eyes full of love, and my heart became whole for what felt like the very first time.

"Make that bacon and you've got a deal."

"Bacon!" Hannah squealed.

"What do you think?" she asked Travis out of the corner of her mouth while holding my gaze.

Travis chuckled and looked up at his mother. "I could eat some bacon."

Her lips twitched. "You've got a deal. Now, return the hostage unharmed."

I released Ian. "Kids, go see if Charlotte has any whipped cream in her fridge."

"Yes!" Hannah yelled, sprinting from the room, Travis hot on her heels.

"If we use all the whipped cream for pancakes, we won't have any for tonight," she teased when we heard the kids celebrating their victory in the kitchen.

Hooking an arm around her shoulders, I pulled her against my chest and then planted a kiss on her mouth. "I'll stock my fridge with whipped cream, you kinky minx."

She grinned. "If it's at your house, it won't do us much good."

"Come back to my place tonight," I whispered.

Her eyes flared with alarm. "Porter—"

"Listen, it's just for one night. Let the kids have a night of normalcy."

"But that's not normal anymore," she argued. "It's not ever going back to the way it was. You can't get them attached to that."

"The new normal is me and you together. Whether that be at my house or at your house. It doesn't matter. This...right here"—I pointedly tightened my arm around her—"is what I want them to get used to."

"But what about the protection order?"

"Exactly. We'll be safer at my house. Here, anyone could stop by. At my place, worst case is my mom shows up and gets to see her grandson. She's not going to rat us out. And I know for a fact that you can't say that same thing about anyone in your family."

She stared at her feet. "I don't know, Porter. Going back to your place…"

"Back when the kids were a real issue for you, I used to dream about having you in my home. The kids fighting around us while you and I cook dinner in the kitchen."

"You mean while I cook dinner in your kitchen," she smarted. "You forget I've seen your culinary skills in action. I probably still have the burn marks to show for it."

I smirked. "Yes, that's exactly what I meant. But I'm more than willing to sit on the counter and cheer you on." I dipped and kissed her. "I want you in my home, Charlotte. I want the kids to sleep in their own beds, even for just one night. And I want to sleep in a room with a door and a bed so, if the mood strikes you, we can seriously utilize one of the twenty-seven cans of whipped cream that are now on my grocery list."

She giggled and stared up at me.

Oh, I was in love with Charlotte Mills. No falling about it.

But, with the sentence that followed, I started to question why.

"Can Ian come too?"

"Woman!" I growled at the same time she burst into laughter.

TWELVE

Charlotte

Porter: I got you a Chihuahua for dinner. You're still good with that, right?

I bit my bottom lip and straightened in the seat of my car. I was sitting outside Brady's house, waiting on Travis to finish dinner. Butterflies the likes I'd never experienced fluttered in my stomach.

Me: You really know how to drive a joke into the ground.
Porter: Is that a no?
Me: Did you cook it?
Porter: Are you insane?
Me: I'm dating you, aren't I?
Porter: So I AM your boyfriend?

I smiled, my face actually aching after I'd spent the day

with Porter, Travis, and Hannah (God, that little girl was cute). We laughed more that day than I suspected any of us had in years.

But all good things came to an end.

Around five that afternoon, I'd had to take Travis to Brady's for dinner.

Porter and I had briefed Travis about not mentioning to Brady that his father had spent the night—and especially not that we were going back to his house that night. My boy's smile had stretched so wide at that news that I didn't figure we had anything to worry about.

Me: Who said anything about you being my boyfriend?

Porter: Oh, I'm sorry. I just assumed considering you can't stop thinking about me naked.

Me: This? Again?

Porter: Tell me it's not the truth.

Me: It's not the truth.

Porter: Now, say it again, but this time, leave out the lies.

Me: I worry about your sanity sometimes.

Porter: Fine. But am I naked in your head while you worry?

I barked a laugh and glanced at the clock on the top of my phone. Three more minutes until I could get Travis and head over to Porter's house.

This thing between us was crazy. We had a long way to go before Porter and I could ever have something solid again—or, more accurately, for the first time. But he'd been right in the darkness: As long as we held on to each other, we didn't have

124

to worry about the rest. When we were together, the world didn't just stop—it disappeared. Travis was happy. Porter was happy. I was happy. And, judging by Hannah's squeals of delight when I'd braided her hair that morning, I assumed she was happy too.

Me: You aren't naked… You're wearing a lovely pair of women's underwear.

Porter: Wow. I'm not sure I wanted to know that.

Me: You still want to be naked in my head?

Porter: Maybe… How do I look in them?

Me: Ah…okay. You're that type of guy. With a name like Porter Reese, I should have seen this coming.

Porter: Damn straight. That's a sexy name.

Me: My mother always warned me about dating men with two first names.

Porter: What the hell kind of blasphemy is that?

Me: I don't know, but now that I know you're considering how well you'd fill out a pair of my panties, it's making me wonder if she wasn't right.

Porter: Well, you're in luck. Your boyfriend also has two LAST names.

Me: Annnndddd…we're right back to the boyfriend thing.

Porter: Yep. But look, it's seven. Go get our boy and then get your sexy ass over here.

My stomach dipped, and I nearly dropped my phone.

Our boy.

My chest got impossibly warm, the words wiggling deep

125

under my skin until they were stroking my soul.

That's who he was.

Ours.

Porter hadn't been there the day he had been born.

And I hadn't been there when he had grown up.

But, as a team, one of us had always been there. First for Lucas, and then for Travis.

Tears pricked the backs of my eyes, the words *I love you* all but clawing their way up my throat. I tamped them down.

Me: Are you going to be wearing women's underwear when I get there?

Porter: Not a chance in hell.

I smiled and swung my car door open. I was halfway up to the door when my phone buzzed in my hand.

Porter: And, as soon as the kids go to sleep, you won't be wearing any, either.

That warmth in my chest traveled south.

Travis chose that exact moment to come barreling out the front door. I jumped and, with pink cheeks, tucked my phone into my pocket.

"Charlotte!" Travis yelled, nearly plowing me over. "Can we go back to your *apartment* now?" He winked, which was more like a blink.

My lips immediately thinned, and I allowed my gaze to drift over his shoulder to where Brady was standing, his shoulder propped against the doorjamb, a hard scowl aimed at me.

Shit.

I was in no mood to go toe to toe with Brady. I was happy, really and truly, for the first time in nearly a decade. And I refused to allow him to ruin that for me.

But just because I refused didn't mean it wasn't going to happen anyway.

"Hey, we need to talk," he called out.

I groaned internally. "Go wait in the car, Trav. I'll be there in a minute."

"Front seat?" he asked.

I gave him a side-eye. He asked that question every time we walked out my front door.

And, every time, I answered with, "Back seat."

Poor kid was lucky I didn't make him sit in a booster seat. Forget about riding in the front.

"Aw, man," he complained and then took off toward my car.

With all the enthusiasm of a snail, I walked over to Brady.

"What's up?" I asked, praying that Travis had been as good as I'd thought he'd been about keeping our little Porter secret.

Brady shoved a hand into the pocket of his jeans. "I want him overnight this weekend."

My shoulders snapped back, and my body went on alert. "What? No way!"

He cocked his head to the side. "I'm not asking. You've had him every night since he's been back."

I crossed my arms over my chest and glared. "Yeah, Brady. Because he's *sick*. He wakes up two to three times a night for breathing treatments and other medication. We both know I'm better equipped to handle that than you are. It's best if he stays with me. Look, you can have him Saturday during the day, but he's coming home with me on Saturday night."

He caught my elbow and yanked me toward him. "Then *teach* me."

"Have you lost your mind?" I hissed, snatching my arm away. "Don't touch me."

Shame flashed in his eyes. He raked a hand through the top of his hair and then cupped the back of his neck. "Shit. I'm sorry."

And, as if Brady's apology hadn't been shocking enough, he lifted his gaze to mine, the grief and dejection almost knocking me back a step.

"I need more time with him. He's not connecting with me like he is with you. He was here for all of two hours tonight. And an hour and a half of that was spent asking when you were coming back to get him."

Guilt settled heavily in my belly. "Brady...I..."

"What am I doing wrong?"

Keeping him from Porter.

"It's only been a week. Be patient."

"It took him, like, ten minutes to warm up to you, Charlotte."

I cut my gaze to the ground. "He'd seen me with Porter. It was built-in trust."

"Jesus," he breathed, tipping his chin toward my car. "He can't get out of here fast enough."

Following his gaze, I found Travis frantically waving for me to come on.

Suddenly, I felt like a heel.

Travis didn't want to leave Brady's; he just wanted to go

home—to Porter's.

I gave Brady's forearm a squeeze. "I'll talk to him. Okay?"

"Yeah. Sure. I'll see you tomorrow." He waved, and before I even had a chance to move, he shut the door.

Every light in the room was on. My head was thrown back against the pillow, my hand in the top of Porter's hair, his mouth between my legs.

It should be noted that, while bathroom sex was amazing, a bed definitely had its merits. The best of which being the ease in which Porter could trail his mouth over every inch of my body.

A strangled cry escaped my throat as his fingers roughly filled me while his tongue swirled over my clit.

"Porter, please," I begged, tugging at his hair.

"Not until you come again," he rumbled, the vibrations doing some seriously nice things.

"I can't, bab—oh God." What started as a whisper morphed into a moan when he twisted his fingers, curling them inside me.

When Travis and I had arrived at the house, a set of nerves I'd never even considered had exploded within me.

Porter had been waiting on the porch for us. But, while looking up at that two-story brick home, I found myself dreading getting out of the car. How was I supposed to walk into that house without feeling like an intruder?

That house was a portal to an entirely different dimension.

A gateway to the world in which my son had grown up.

A world where he called another woman mom.

The same woman who had taken him from me.

Numbly, I'd accepted a kiss from Porter before he'd guided me inside. One step through the door and I realized that it was worse than I'd feared. Images of my son covered the walls in a weird yet charming hodgepodge of frames. As much as I wanted to investigate, memorize, and absorb every one of those stolen moments from his childhood, I couldn't bring myself to look.

What if she was in the pictures? Holding my son. Smiling with my son. Laughing with my son. Living and enjoying every moment she'd robbed me of.

I'd told myself that the past didn't matter, but it still felt like a dozen copies of his deep-brown eyes were boring into me from all angles, taunting me with memories I'd never have.

So I pretended those pictures didn't exist.

Only they became all I could think about.

Curiosity consumed me while self-preservation waged its war.

I smiled on cue. Laughed when something was funny. Held on to Porter as if he could make it stop. But I never opened my mouth to tell him why I was silently losing my mind.

It wasn't his fault that Catherine had turned out to be a madwoman. But being there, where she had once lived, was smothering me.

After eating a takeout dinner from The Porterhouse—on dishes the woman I hated with every fiber of my being had probably bought—we'd spent the night on the couch she'd probably sat on, my legs tangled with a man who had once vowed to love her and my son playing—and fighting—with her daughter.

She had stolen my child and seamlessly slipped him into her dead son's life.

Was I now slipping into her life?

During a movie the kids had insisted we watch, they had fallen asleep.

Porter did not delay in carrying them both to their rooms.

And then carrying *me* to his bed.

Or was it her bed?

Desperate for a distraction from the swirling tornado in my head, I eagerly welcomed his body.

Porter took me long and hard, until we were both covered in a sheen of sweat. But, even after we'd finished, I wasn't ready to go back to reality.

In the shower, I guided his hands between my legs and pretended for a little while longer. Only I couldn't silence my mind long enough to find another release. So, when the hot water had turned to cold, it had forced us, dripping wet, through his bedroom, where he'd planted me on the bed seconds before his mouth disappeared between my legs.

"Porter," I cried as he worked me closer and closer to the edge. I fisted the sheets and rolled my hips against his mouth. My whole body was coiled tight.

Porter never slowed his torturous tongue or his magical fingers.

"Oh God," I moaned as my orgasm finally sprang to the surface, demolishing me in its wake.

I fell back on the bed, my heart racing but every other muscle in my body going slack.

All except my mind.

How many times had he done that with her?

I slapped a hand over my mouth as the thought assaulted me.

Closing my eyes, I counted backward from twenty, trying to trick my brain into some sort of semblance of calm.

None was found.

"You feeling any better now?" he asked, collapsing beside me on the bed.

Folding my arm over my face, I hid from him.

He moved my arm and searched my face. "Do I need to turn the lights off for you to talk to me?"

"W…what?" I stammered, the promise of the darkness almost as exciting as it was terrifying.

He would have made me feel better in the darkness, but in order to get that, I would have had to confess the landfill of garbage in my head.

He scooted in close and rested his hand on my hip. "You've been stuck in your head all night."

I twisted my lips. "No. I haven't."

"Really?" he drawled, arching an eyebrow. "You stared at the wall for over an hour earlier."

"I'm not a movie person," I defended.

"Yeah, but you didn't stare at me like you usually do when you get bored."

I attempted humor. "Jesus, Porter. I'm not that creepy."

"You *are* that creepy. And I fucking love it. But, tonight, you were off in your own little world." He pecked me on the lips and smiled. "And you didn't even invite me to come with you."

Unable to reply around the lump in my throat, I inched

132

into his space until he rolled to his back and tucked me into his side so my head was resting on his chest.

My breathing shuddered as I fought to keep my emotions beneath the surface.

"Jesus, Charlotte," he whispered, but he didn't push to make me explain.

His fingers played in my hair as mine gripped his arm impossibly tight while I forced myself to stay in that moment with him and not disappear into the past.

His mouth came to the top of my hair, where he kissed me. "Was tonight too much for you? Like, with the kids?"

I tilted my head back to see him, a pang of guilt hitting my stomach when I saw the worry carved in his face. "No. The kids were great. I love seeing him happy. And Hannah's a doll."

He blew out a relieved breath. "Good. Okay. So, was Brady a dick when you picked up Travis?"

I cut my gaze to the corner. "He started to be, but then I realized he's just sad. Travis isn't really giving him much of a chance."

"Yeah. He's not Brady's biggest fan. Apparently, Brady's been talking shit about you to his wife."

I scoffed. "Well, that's nothing new."

His jaw became hard. "Maybe not, but it's a problem when my son overhears it. He's got to cut that shit out if he wants any hope of a relationship with Travis. You're his mother. And, if he was any kind of man, he'd respect that and try to reinforce that bond, not tear it down."

My mouth was so fast that my mind didn't have the chance to filter my rough tone before I'd released the words into the wild. "Is that what you're planning to do for Hannah?"

His chin snapped to the side. "What?"

I clamped my mouth shut and rolled away.

"Charlotte, what the hell?" he questioned as I started yanking my clothes up off the floor.

I gave him my back so he couldn't read the lie on my face. "Travis and I need to get home."

"It's one in the morning, and you told him you were spending the night."

When I heard the mattress creak, I hurried to get my shirt over my head before he could stop me.

"Yeah, but I just remembered—"

The room plunged into darkness, which sent a tsunami of panic crashing down over me. I didn't want Catherine in the darkness. That was mine and she couldn't have it.

"No. Turn them back on! Turn them back on! Turn them back on!"

Blessed light flooded the room, and my whole body trembled with relief.

"What the hell is going on?" he rumbled.

"I have to go home," I choked out, rushing to my shoes and slipping them on.

I hadn't made it more than two steps when he suddenly wrapped me up in a hug.

"You have to talk to me."

"Porter, stop," I cried.

He let me go, but then he stepped in front of me, blocking my path to the door. "Let me in, Charlotte."

"I need to leave."

He shook his head and planted his hands on his hips. "Whatever the fuck that has been poisoning your head all night, you gotta give it to me, sweetheart. I can't fix it if I don't know what it is."

My eyes welled with tears. He was right. She was poisoning me. She'd already ruined my life. And, now, she was about to ruin my relationship with Porter too.

"I have to…get away from her," I admitted.

"Who?" he breathed, taking a step toward me, his hands going to my hips and pulling me close.

"Catherine," I croaked.

His hands spasmed, but his face softened. "Baby, she's not here."

"She raised my child in this house, Porter. I can't do this. I didn't think about it before I agreed to come here. But it's all I've been able to think about."

He blew out a loud and long exhale. "Come with me, Charlotte."

I shook my head, but when he took my hand and intertwined our fingers, I had no choice but to follow him.

Shirtless and in only a pair of pajama pants, he led me through the house and out the front door.

"Porter, the kids. We can't leave."

"We're not going anywhere," he said. After guiding me to the curb, he stepped behind me and then pointed to a cute one-story brick house at the end of the cul-de-sac. "That was the house Catherine and I bought together."

"What?" I breathed.

He shifted my back closer to his front and rested his chin on the top of my head. "Remember the day at Tanner's pond when I tried to pick a fight with the water? Well, that was the day the kids and I moved out. I didn't have this one yet, but

I refused to stay in that house anymore. Her deceit was suffocating me, no matter how hard I tried to move on. I'd been doing my best to keep the kids' lives stable after losing her, but I couldn't close my eyes without seeing her holding him underwater. We moved into my parents' house while I debated on what to do. I wanted to keep Travis in the same school district, and back then, he had a few friends in the neighborhood. The minute this house came on the market, I bought it sight unseen."

He turned me in his arms and dropped his forehead to mine. "Outside of a few things in the kids' bedrooms, there's nothing in my house of Catherine's. For the last three years, I kept a picture on my dresser of her holding Travis as a baby." He paused before correcting himself. "The real Travis, not your Lucas. I left it there so the kids wouldn't have to feel like they had to erase her from their lives too. But, last week, when I got home from the police station, I shattered it against the wall."

My breathing shuddered, and I looped my arms around his neck. "I hate her so much for what she did. She ruined my life, Porter. She took the only thing I would have died to keep."

"And I will never fault you for that. I hate her too. But there's still a small part of me that feels guilty for not recognizing that she had some serious psychological problems. Christ, Charlotte. I would have saved us all a lot of heartache if—"

I slapped a hand over his mouth. "Don't do that. That's the what-if vortex that will swallow you whole if you let it. Don't go there, Porter. Stay with me."

He swayed into me as his eyes turned to glass.

I held his stare until he nodded.

Removing my hand from his mouth, I confessed, "I felt like I was slipping into her life tonight."

"Jesus, Charlotte. That's some heavy shit. Why didn't you say anything?"

I shrugged. "Because it wouldn't have been your fault. I don't know. I was blamed for a lot of years for something I couldn't change. I guess I didn't want to do that to you."

He hugged me tighter. "I *never* would have asked you to come over here tonight if there was even a tinge of her anywhere in my house. Hannah is all there is left of Catherine in my life and she's the *only* part of that woman I will ever expect you to accept."

"It's not Hannah's fault. She is an innocent little girl, Porter."

"I'm really fucking glad you feel that way. Because every time she got near you tonight, I worried that she was overwhelming you. I love you, Charlotte. But that's my daughter."

"Porter. Hannah doesn't bother me at all. And if she did...I would have left. I would never put you in a situation where you had to choose. It's why, back when I was struggling with the fact that you had children, I was trying so hard to figure out a way to be okay with it. I know you love your kids." I pressed a slow and reverent kiss to his lips. "And, if you want the truth, it might be the biggest reason why I love you. In a world where people told me to move on and let go, with you, I didn't have to feel guilty for still loving my son as much as I did because, if you were in my shoes, you would have been just as devastated."

He blew out a heavy groan. "In a way, I was in your shoes for a week and I almost broke. I have no idea how you did it for so long."

"I don't know, either. But it's over now." I pressed up onto my toes and whispered against his lips, "For both of us."

"I still have Catherine's stuff," he admitted. "It's in a storage unit across town. Everything from our furniture to her clothes. Picture albums, knickknacks. Whatever. I kept it all for the kids in case they ever want any of it. Especially Hannah. Are you going to be able to live with that if it happens one day?"

My breath caught in my throat. "That's a long way in the future, Porter."

"But it's in the future, Charlotte. And, if this thing with us works out, it's going to be in *your* future. And what about Travis?"

My body turned to granite, and my heart stopped at the very idea. "You think he'd want some of her stuff?"

"Now? No. He remembers being in the car with her. But he still loved her at one time. And I think, the older he gets and the closer he gets to you, the more he'll realize how terrible the things she did really were. But I can't swear that to you for sure."

I chewed on my bottom lip. "I don't know how I would ever handle that."

He kissed my temple and murmured, "It's not his fault, either. Just start preparing in case it ever happens. Every now and again, he'll talk about her. It's rare. But it does happen."

I nodded and then buried my face in his chest, sending up a dozen prayers that that day would never come. We stood there for several minutes in the darkness, the light of the moon and the stars bearing down on us.

"So, can I talk to you about something serious right now?"

he murmured.

I popped my head up. "More serious than your ex who kidnapped my son?"

He grinned. "Yes."

"This doesn't sound good."

He trailed his hands down until they splayed over my ass. "Relax. It's good. I promise. At least, for me, anyway."

"Great," I smarted.

He chuckled and bent low until his lips were at my ear, where he whispered, "You said you love me."

My stomach dipped. "No. I didn't."

His grin became a full-blown smile. "Yeah, you did. You said that you knew I loved my kids and that was the biggest reason you love me."

I huffed and rolled my eyes. "I meant…the biggest reason why I was *falling* in love with you."

"Still?" he complained.

A laugh escaped my throat before I was able to stop it. "It's only been a night, Porter. Remember, with a man like you, it's a *really long* trip."

He narrowed his eyes and hissed, "Liar."

And I was. Because there wasn't a man in the entire world who would ever be able to compare to Porter.

Not his warmth.

Not his understanding.

Not his heart.

And definitely not the way he loved.

So, for that reason alone, I looked up at him and whispered, "I am. Wholly and completely."

He tipped his head to the side and arched an eyebrow.

"Was that a riddle? You are what? A liar or in love with me?"

I shrugged. "I guess we'll never know."

Porter's glare turned murderous, but his mouth split into a smile that stole my breath.

Less than a second later, the ground disappeared from beneath my feet and I found myself slung over his shoulder.

Laughing, he carried me back into the house.

I did my best to keep my giggles soft as he toted me down the hall and into the bedroom.

And then both of our laughter stopped when his mouth covered mine.

Twenty minutes later, as we lay sated in a tangled heap, I told Porter once and for all that I loved him.

He stared deep into my eyes, a million emotions cascading through his handsome features, and replied, "Too late now. I've already moved on."

He was seriously insane.

But it was safe to say I was, in fact, wholly and completely in love with that man.

THIRTEEN

Porter

"WHAT IF THEY HATE ME?" SHE ASKED.

I took her hand in mine and laced our fingers together. "Oh, my mom definitely will."

Her head snapped up. "Porter!"

Laughing, I kept my gaze aimed out the windshield and gave her a reassuring squeeze. "You didn't let me finish. I meant, she'll hate you for about ten seconds until she sees him and then she'll love you."

Charlotte looked at the kids in the back seat. Hannah was sound asleep in her car seat, as she was so often when we were in the car. Travis was sitting beside her, peering out the window, an epic smile covering his face.

He'd been smiling like that for a week.

And, soon enough, he'd be able to smile like that permanently.

For the last seven days, Charlotte and I had been playing

a dangerous game. We were still a week out from a court date when we could hopefully have the order of protection lifted. However, we weren't letting it stop us.

Since the day Charlotte had first called me to come over, there hadn't been a night we hadn't fallen asleep together. Half of those nights, when she had been positive no one would be stopping by, we'd stayed at her apartment. The other half, we'd stayed at my house. But it didn't matter where we rested our heads. All that mattered was that we were doing it together.

And God, was I happy.

Every day, she laughed. Every day, my kids smiled. And, every day, I fell more and more in love with a life I desperately wanted to keep.

"Are you sure we should be doing this?" she whispered. "Maybe we should wait until after our court date."

I smirked. "Baby, my family is celebrating. That means *you* are celebrating."

"I know, but the police literally just dropped your investigation, like, three hours ago. Maybe we shouldn't push our luck with the law today."

I turned down Tanner's long, oak-covered driveway. "There was no luck involved in this. Quit stressing. We're safe here. My parents aren't going to be alerting the authorities."

"I don't know," she mumbled. "It feels—"

"*Good.* That's the word you're looking for." I smirked and shot her a wink. "But, if you think it feels good now, wait until you see me in a bathing suit."

She'd been winding herself up since I'd told her that my family was having an impromptu cookout to celebrate my release from potential jailbird status. I'd yet to tell any of them about Charlotte and me being back together. And, since I hadn't left her side at all, I'd been avoiding them. In that time, Travis hadn't stopped asking about my parents or Tanner. Today seemed like a great opportunity to kill two birds with one surprise stone. And, with the temperatures well into the nineties, it was the perfect time to break Tanner's pond in for the season.

Glaring at me, she asked, "It's that bad, huh?"

"Bad?" My mouth fell open in mock horror. "Sweetheart, I fill out a pink Speedo better than any man you've ever seen."

She blinked, her beautiful face completely blank. "Please, God, tell me you're kidding."

I was. But she knew that.

"Nope."

"I'm such a lucky girl," she deadpanned.

I lifted our joined hands to my lips and kissed her knuckles. "And don't you forget it."

"Hannie, wake up. We're here!" Travis exclaimed as I put the car into park.

"Yay," she croaked before her lids were even open.

I glanced to Charlotte who was staring up at the tall plantation house, nerves crinkling the corners of her eyes.

"It's going to be fine," I told her.

"You should have warned them that I was coming," she whispered as the kids scrambled out of the car.

"And ruin the surprise? No way."

She licked her lips and turned her panic-filled gaze on me. "I don't want to be the surprise."

I barked a laugh and slung my door open. "Good, little miss self-centered, because you're not. *He* is. They probably won't even notice you're here for the first hour."

"Right," she whispered but made no move to get out of the car.

With two fingers, I brushed her long hair off her neck. "Charlotte, my parents are good people. They have two sons. They know what you've been through. They aren't going to judge you for the way things have gone down recently."

"I know… I just feel like the enemy in their eyes."

Travis knocked on her window. "Charlotte, let's go! I'm going to teach you how to fish." He grinned and lifted his blue-and-white tackle box.

Keeping my voice low so Travis couldn't hear me, I told her, "You aren't the enemy in my eyes or in his eyes, and the minute my family sees that, they will become the only eyes that matter."

She sucked in a deep breath and blew it out with practiced control. "Okay. You're right."

"Mmm," I purred. "Stop trying to seduce me with sexy words like that and let's meet my parents."

She laughed, and it curled over my skin like the sweetest touch. I'd never get enough of that from her.

Shoving her door open, she stepped out of the car. Travis immediately took her hand and started dragging her around the side of the house. After scooping Hannah off her feet and planting her on my hip, I caught up with them and threw my arm around her shoulders.

Together, the four of us walked around the house.

We hadn't made the final curve before the smell of steaks and the sound of Mom and Tanner laughing filled the air in the most amazing combination.

It was home and happiness all wrapped up in one.

Since Tanner had bought that house, we'd had a lot of these cookouts. He always cooked. My mom took care of Hannah. My dad fished with Travis. And I would numbly watch them all while I tried to force the overwhelming hate and anger from my heart.

My life over the last three years had been survived in various degrees of hell.

But not that day. Not with Charlotte at my side. My kids. Her son.

No. There was nothing hellish about that day.

It was pretty damn perfect.

As we made our way toward the stone patio, Tanner saw us first.

"Holy. Shit," he said behind a giant stainless-steel commercial grill that had cost him a small fortune.

"What?" Mom chirped from the picnic table as she stirred what I prayed was her bacon ranch pasta salad. Her head slowly lifted to my brother, but her eyes found mine on the way up. She started to smile, but her gaze slipped to Charlotte and then down to Travis.

"Oh, thank you, God," she cried, slapping her hands over her mouth, tears instantly hitting her eyes.

Charlotte's arm tensed around me, but I held her tight and whispered, "Relax. She always reacts like this when she sees me."

Charlotte suddenly came to an abrupt stop. "I don't know about this, Porter."

"It's fine. I swear."

My mom screamed for my dad as she and Tanner

abandoned the food and raced toward us.

She went straight for Travis, bending low to pull him in for a hug. "Wow, I've been missing you."

Tanner extended a hand my way. I clasped it, and he pulled me in for a quick back pat and whispered, "Do I even want to know how you pulled this off?"

I chuckled. "Probably not."

As he stepped away, he took Hannah from my arms and tickled her stomach. "What's up with you, sweet girl?"

"Nothing," she said casually, as though it hadn't been the most chaotic two weeks of her life. "Where are my floaties? I'm ready to swim."

"Awesome. Good chat." Tanner laughed and put her on her feet. "Nana bought you a brand-new set for this year. Go look on the kitchen table. And tell Grandpa to turn the TV off and come outside."

I smiled, watching her trot away in a pink-and-purple-striped bathing suit complete with a white tutu.

When I glanced back at my brother, he was staring at Charlotte, his smile smug.

I pulled her deeper into my side. "You remember Charlotte, right?"

He nodded. "I sure do."

"Sloth," she greeted.

His eyebrows shot up. "We're still on that?"

"The truth doesn't expire," she retorted.

He chuckled and looked at his feet while shaking his head. "Well, your obviously impaired vision aside, I'm glad you're here."

She swallowed hard and then looked up at me. Her brown

eyes were filled with concern, but she whispered, "I'm glad I'm here too."

"Come on, Nana. Stop." Travis laughed, wiggling in her embrace.

She reluctantly released him. "Excuse me. I haven't seen you in *two* weeks. I do believe I'm due for more than one hug."

"You got, like, a million, so..." he grumbled.

"A million and one never hurt anyone," she argued, smiling.

"Mom?" I called.

Her head snapped up, but her focus didn't come to me. It went to the woman in my arms.

"Hi there," my mom whispered.

"Hi," Charlotte replied, equally as quiet.

"Charlotte, this is my mom, Lynn Reese. Mom, this is my *girlfriend*, Charlotte Mills."

"Dad!" Travis scolded. "You know she hates it when you call her your girlfriend."

I lifted a finger in the air and corrected, "No. She hates it when I refer to myself as her boyfriend. She adores it when I call her my girlfriend."

"Actually," Charlotte started.

"Nope! I reject your complaints today. This is a celebration in *my* honor."

She rolled her eyes and then looked to my mother. "I'm sorry. I'm relatively new to this parenting thing, but if you happen to have any advice on how we can prevent Travis from turning out as goofy as Porter, I'd be open to hearing more about that."

My mother was an amazing woman. The kind who

passed Popsicles out to the neighborhood kids on hot summer days. She volunteered with elderly patients at various nursing homes across the city. And, every year, she prepared hundreds of hygiene kits for the local homeless shelter. When Catherine died, she'd stepped up in a huge way to help me. She'd put her whole life on hold for my kids. She took Travis to doctors' appointments when I had to work and taught Hannah how to spell her name by the time she was two. She was warm and thoughtful. Generous and kind.

All of which explains why I was so taken aback by the icy chill in her tone when she snipped at Charlotte.

"We? How *we* can prevent Travis from being as goofy as my son?"

"Whoa. Whoa. Whoa." I released Charlotte and stepped forward. "Let's bring the attitude down a notch. Yeah?"

Her gaze never came to mine. Instead, it narrowed on Charlotte. "Answer me."

Charlotte's face paled. "I…uh… It was a joke. I didn't mean to imply that Porter isn't a great man. Sometimes my humor…is a little…"

My mom opened her mouth, but I got there first.

"Hey, Travis? Why don't you go help Uncle Tanner cook."

"Yeah… Let's, uh…do that," Tanner replied, staring at my mom like she had grown a third head.

Travis glanced back and forth between his grandmother and his mother. "Um…okay."

As soon as he was out of earshot, I fisted a hand on my hip and glared at my mother. "Don't do that again. I don't care what kind of issue you have. You don't lay them out in front of him. He's been through enough without adding your stress on top of it."

My mom's eyes finally flicked to mine, and she nodded sheepishly. "You're right. I'm sorry."

I blew out a ragged breath, and my shoulders sagged. "Christ. Can we please drop the drama for one damn day?"

"Fine. But I need to know if she was serious about the *we* part?"

Charlotte shook her head. "I'm sorry, I don't know what you mean."

"I'm asking if you're going to let us be a part of his life. Or if this is just a visit. I deserve to know. I have no idea what is going on right now..." Her voice broke as her anger slipped. "But I need to know how to prepare myself for when today ends."

Fuck. Okay. Perhaps Charlotte had been right and I should have told them she was coming *and* given them an up-date on the last week and our whole *together* thing.

"Okay. And *I* will give you that information, but lay off Char—"

"It's okay, Porter," Charlotte said, catching my arm. Stepping around me, she straightened her back and squared her shoulders. "Mrs. Reese, I can understand your hesitance about me. Quite honestly, I was hesitant about coming here today too. I feared I'd be seen exactly the way you are looking at me now. As some sort of person who snatched your grand-son away from you. Porter's an amazing man, but I think his love for me has blinded him to how truly unique our situ-ation is for everyone involved. All of us have had our lives rocked due to the decisions that were made for us without our knowledge or our consent. I didn't want to lose Lucas ten years ago any more than you wanted to lose Travis two weeks ago. But both things happened and neither of us are at fault for that."

She sucked in a breath, the color slowly creeping back into her cheeks. "I'm sure you remember that first day at Porter's house when I realized Travis was my son. It wasn't pretty. But it was definitely real. I love him. As I know you do too. Tanner told me the other day that Travis was the answer to all of our questions. So yeah, we're here today because Travis wanted to come. And, regardless what happens with Porter and me, I can tell you with absolute honesty that, as long as Travis wants you and your family in his life, that is where you will be."

By the time she finished, my heart was in my throat and pride flowed through my veins.

Hooking an arm around her shoulders, I pulled her into my side and kissed the top of her head.

"Well," my mom breathed, lifting a shaking hand up to smooth her short, blond hair down. "I may have underestimated my son's taste in women."

"Gee, thanks," I mumbled.

"And I'm sorry." She looked away as the tears started to spill from her eyes. "Sorry for my snap judgment. Sorry I made you uncomfortable. Sorry you've had your life flipped upside down by all of this too. And, most of all, I'm sorry you lost your son." She stared Charlotte directly in the eye, tears glistening on her cheeks. "But…it has been the absolute joy of my life, helping raise that little boy over the last few years, so thank you for allowing me to continue to do that."

"Jesus," I breathed, hooking my other arm out and dragging my mom into my other side.

Yeah...I definitely should have warned them she was coming.

"Wow. You sure know how to bring the party, Porter," Tanner said, strolling back over. "You've got Mom crying. Your girlfriend's crying. And Dad just burst into tears when he saw Travis. I swear—you keep this shit up and I'm not inviting you next time."

Mom sniffled and stepped out of my arms. "You're right. This is a celebration. Especially now that Travis is back." She gave Charlotte's shoulder a squeeze and then moved to my brother, linking her arm through his. "All right. Let's get back to cooking. We need two more steaks and at least one more side. But it has to be quick because Hannah is *not* going to wait long before hitting the pond."

Tanner winked as they meandered away, discussions of Tabbouleh salad ringing in the air.

Alone, I shifted Charlotte in my arms so her front was pressed to mine and whispered, "That was amazing."

Craning her head back, she said, "You are officially fired as the communications manager for our relationship."

"What? Why? I think that went great."

Her mouth fell open, and she lifted her fingers in the shape of a telephone to her mouth and ear. And then, in a deep, ridiculous voice that sounded nothing like mine, she mocked, "Hey, Mom, I'm bringing Charlotte with me to the cookout. She and I are in a relationship and have committed to doing what's best for Travis. Uh huh. Yes. Of course he'll be there too. Okay, sounds great. See you then." She hung up her pretend phone and glared at me.

I twisted my lips. "Okay. Fine. I'll admit that might have

been the best course of action. But, sweetheart, I assure you your fancy-ass speech was way better. I'm pretty sure my mom fell in love with you by the end of it."

She shook her head before hissing, "Fired!"

"Okay. I'm sorry. You were right. And that's not me trying to seduce you. Though…there is a really good chance of you getting some tonight."

She rolled her eyes. "Just a heads-up. Whenever we do come out of the closet with this to *my* family, I'm totally throwing you to the wolves." She quirked an eyebrow before finishing with, "And Tom carries a gun."

I barked a laugh then touched my lips to hers. "You ready to meet my dad? He's gonna *love* you."

She glowered.

But it was beautiful.

If for no other reason than it was aimed at me.

FOURTEEN

Charlotte

AFTER THE WORLD'S MOST AWKWARD INTRODUCTIONS that left me wishing I had sent Porter's family gift cards in lieu of attending the cookout, the rest of the day was actually a lot of fun.

By the time I met Tommy Reese, he'd gotten the rundown of what was going on between Porter and me. He greeted me with a huge smile that looked just like his sons' and an even bigger hug.

He talked.

I listened.

And Porter never left my side.

Slowly but surely, I started to relax.

After our showdown of sorts, it was as if a switch had been flipped and Lynn seemed to take to me. I was a relatively quiet person, but she was having none of it. She asked about my family, my career, and my friends. And, in turn, she told me about her family, her career, and her friends.

She'd almost dropped a plate when she'd found out Rita was my best friend. It seemed Tanner was a momma's boy, because she knew entirely too much about his relationship with Rita. To hear Lynn tell it, her son had been smitten, planning lavish vacations, and introducing Rita to all of his celebrity friends. She'd told me that the two of them hadn't spoken again since Tanner had shown up at my apartment and unleashed on me the morning after I'd gotten Lucas back. Lynn worried that Tanner was nothing more than a pretty-faced rebound for my best friend. I thought this was probably true but made a mental note to call Rita and see what was really going on.

Lunch had been amazing. It was clear Tanner had inherited his culinary skills from his mother. His steaks were unbelievable, but her bacon ranch pasta salad was to die for. And, after watching Porter eat his fourth mountainous plate of it, I feared that was exactly what was going to happen. Over lunch, the guys reminisced about their rowdy youth. I literally couldn't stop laughing as Porter recounted stories of how his father had made him cut the grass with a pair of scissors after he'd gotten caught skipping math class in junior high. And Tanner told me that he'd been forced to wash his dad's Corvette with a toothbrush after he'd gotten caught with his first girlfriend in his bedroom.

Through it all, I couldn't help but feel that warmth in my chest spiraling out of control, because for as much as I was laughing, so was Travis. He even stopped Tanner a time or two to correct the details of his uncle's story. Clearly, it wasn't the first time he'd heard them, and I loved the idea that he'd grown up with that feeling of warmth and belonging.

Once we'd finished eating, the kids took off to the corn hole boards for a game, and during that time, we discussed Travis's health in great detail. Lynn asked me at least a dozen questions, and Tanner and Tommy listened intently to my answers. Porter chimed in several times, but for the most part, he sat back, anchored his hand to my thigh, and let me brief his family.

While I was sure Travis would have loved to swim with his little sister, excessive exercise wasn't good for his heart. Something it seemed the Reese family not only knew, but had been mitigating for years. As soon as Hannah waded into the water, yelling for her father and Uncle Tan, Tommy took his grandson down to the dock on the opposite end of the pond to go fishing.

I sat there for hours, watching everyone interact with each other. The smiles were smooth and effortless. And the love was beautiful and refreshing.

Good people did exist. The Reese family was proof.

And it stirred emotions inside me that left my mind reeling.

"You're still refusing to swim?" Porter asked as he sauntered over to me. His bathing suit—thankfully a pair of board shorts and not a pink Speedo—was dripping and his wet hair hung down over his forehead.

"Did you see the size of the fish Travis caught a minute ago? I'm concerned its cousin the Loch Ness monster might show up for revenge at any minute."

He chuckled and sank onto the grassy bank beside me. "You doing okay over here?"

"Yeah. Today was fun."

He looped his arms though mine and folded our hands together, resting them on his thigh. "I told you it would be."

Hannah's laughter rang through the air as Tanner ducked under the water and pretended to be a shark.

"Your family is crazy. I see where you get it from."

He scooted closer until our thighs were touching. "Is that why you're over here, looking like you are on the verge of a panic attack?"

I tore my gaze off my son, who was casting a line into the water at the other end of the pond. "What?"

"Come on. Don't bullshit me. You've been happy all day, and for the last thirty minutes, you've been sitting over here alone, staring up at the sky like you're waiting for it to fall."

Wow. That was…surprisingly accurate.

Though I wasn't waiting for the sky to fall, I'd been trying to make heads or tails of how perfect it felt.

Everything was too right. Too good. Too temporary.

I didn't get those things in life. Yet, right then, I had them all.

And it scared the hell out of me.

At my silence, his eyes flashed dark. "You want to talk about it?"

"I can't decide if we're too real or not real enough," I whispered.

His body locked up tight. "Confessional?"

"No," I said. "Not here. Not tonight. Let's just talk."

He cleared his throat and stared at me. "Then I'm going to tell you, first and foremost, there is no such thing as too real or not real enough. There's just real. And there's just us."

Guilt slashed through me. "I don't mean for it to sound

like that. I wasn't talking about us. Well, not completely, anyway. It's… Today was so great it almost made me uncomfortable. I'm starting to think I don't know how to be happy. Is that, like, normal in a situation like this?"

"Charlotte, there is nothing normal about us."

"Right. I know that. But are *you* happy?"

"Today? Unquestionably."

"See, for me, it's like I go through these spurts where I'm really happy, and then I realize I'm happy and it scares me because I'm well versed in how quickly that can be taken away."

"I get it, baby. We've lived through a lot of sour over the years. But this is the sweet. Remember when I told you I used to come here every year and get in the water, trying to figure out how to let go?"

My chest tightened, but not a single word made it to my tongue, so I nodded.

He pressed a kiss to my forehead, allowing his lips to linger for several beats. "One dip in that pond, knowing you were sitting on the bank, my boy down on the dock, fishing with his grandpa, my daughter playing with her grandmother and her uncle, and I didn't just figure out how to let go—I felt the pain disappear."

"See, rational thought tells me that it's impossible to find the energy to feed the pain and hate when you're surrounded by so much goodness and love. And yet I can't seem to relax. No matter how good it is. It's like I've been programmed for the darkness and I'm lost in the light."

"Sweetheart," he purred in understanding.

I looked at the water. "I love this life. I've never been happier than I have been in the last week. I close my eyes at night, knowing when I open them you're still going to be there. I still stress and worry about losing Travis, but it's manageable with you. I, as a general rule, don't like people."

He chuckled, but I wasn't joking.

"I don't, Porter. But I *love* you. And I *love* that *he* loves you. And then, today, you bring me to meet your family." I paused when the emotion of my confession became too much. But I refused to cry. Not anymore. "And don't think I didn't notice you calling me your girlfriend all day." I laughed and it luckily kept the tears at bay. "But this all scares me so much." I peered up into his blue eyes and asked the question I didn't actually want to know the answer to. "I need to know the truth. I've been doing it for so long. I don't even know what's real anymore. Are we pretending here?"

He grinned. "Are *you* pretending?"

I shook my head. "I don't think so."

"You don't *think* so or you aren't?"

"I…uh…" I stammered.

He chuckled. "Charlotte, are you happy?"

I swallowed hard. "Right this second? Yes. But what about—"

He pinched my lips closed with his thumb and forefinger. "Stop with the buts and what-ifs. If you always expect to get kicked in the stomach, that's all you're ever going to get. There are going to be ups and downs, sweetheart. But you can't let the lows color the highs. You had a good day today, right?"

"Yesh," I mumbled around his fingers.

That damn sexy grin of his grew exponentially. "Good! Then enjoy it. Today, we have it all. And we fucking earned every second of that happiness." One of his hands went under my legs and the other around my back.

I draped my arm over his neck, assuming he was dragging me onto his lap.

He didn't.

He rose to his feet with me in his arms.

"You have to embrace the good times or the bad times will always overwhelm you. When you look back on this day, a year from now, I don't want you to remember the last thirty minutes of fear. I want you to remember laughing and living in the light with people who love you." A smirk tipped the side of his mouth. "And maybe swimming too."

My eyes flashed wide as he took a step toward the pond.

"Porter, don't!" I demanded, squirming in his arms. "There are fish in that pond."

"They aren't piranhas though." He laughed, and that sexy rat bastard just kept walking.

"Please!" I squealed.

"This is as real as life gets," he said, stopping at the edge.

"If you throw me in that water, you are going to wish you were pretending," I snapped, but then I laughed when he started swinging me toward the pond. "Stop! I don't have a change of clothes." I cackled, clinging to his neck.

"How do you feel right now, Charlotte?"

"Like I'm going to kill you."

He laughed. "But you aren't scared, are you?"

"For your safety? Yes," I shot back.

"A year from now, you'll remember this."

"From the inside of a prison cell!"

"Say you love me," he ordered.

I glanced up and saw that everyone had stopped what

they were doing and were now watching us as they smiled. "I love you!" I whisper-yelled. "Now, put me down."

He jerked like he was going to throw me. "Louder."

"Porter!" I hissed. "People are staring at us." I squeaked when he faked me out again.

"Louder."

"Fine. I love you!" I yelled, tucking my face in his neck as my cheeks flashed hot with embarrassment.

"Good. Then you should have no problem forgiving me for this."

"No!" I yelled, but it was too late.

He jumped into the water with me securely held against his chest.

Laughing underwater, I tried desperately not to think of the possibility of a fish brushing my leg and, instead, focused on Porter.

Maybe he was right. We'd been through hell. If ever there were two people who deserved a happily-ever-after, it was us. Happiness was a state of mind, not something you had to hold on to for fear you'd never get it back.

But, for people like us, life wasn't a case of sour and sweet.

It was more like the deepest pits of despair and the high of cloud nine.

And, as my head popped up out of that water, I knew I'd been wrong to ever assume I wasn't still in that pit.

FIFTEEN

Porter

"T RAVIS!" DAD YELLED AS I BREACHED THE SURFACE, A smile splitting my mouth.

The panicked tone of his voice shot through me like an arrow. Treading water, I spun in a circle as Charlotte emerged beside me.

She laughed, oblivious. "I'm going to kill—"

She was cut off by my mom's terror-filled screams.

"Get him! Tommy, get him!"

"What the hell?" I breathed as my sixty-year-old father dove into the pond.

My pulse spiked as my mind struggled to piece the situation together. I couldn't see anything. But maybe that was the most telling of all. The dock, where my son had just been standing, was now completely empty.

"Where's Travis?" Charlotte asked beside me, her voice bearing the slightest of trembles.

And then the world rushed to an immeasurable speed. Slingshotting my life into fast forward while I remained utterly still with no way to catch up.

My dad's hand shot out of the water, catching on the wood beam at the corner of the dock. My son's lifeless body in his arms.

"Help me!" he roared.

Suddenly, my chest caught fire, and less than a second later, my body exploded.

There had been exactly one other time in my life when I'd swung my arms that fast, kicked my legs that frantically, or prayed that hard.

Time moved at an agonizing pace as I once again waged war with the water in that fucking pond. I couldn't remember if I took a breath the entire way, but regardless, my lungs were on the verge of collapsing when I finally reached them. They were worthless to me anyway, because I died a thousand deaths at the sight of my son unconscious and unmoving in my father's arms.

"What the fuck happened?" I barked, wrapping Travis around the shoulders and pulling his back to my front. I bargained with any and every god that he would gasp for breath or start laughing that it was some sort of sick joke.

But he was utterly still.

"I...I don't know," Dad replied. "He was reeling a fish in and just collapsed into the water."

Charlotte finally appeared in the water in front of us. Her face was pale and her hands were shaking as she tried to check for a pulse. "He's not breathing. We have to get him out of here. Now!"

"I'm trying," I replied, struggling to get his limp body up onto the dock, but it was too high for me to be able to lift him.

The tiniest fraction of relief ruptured inside me when Tanner arrived on foot.

"Give him to me!" he shouted, dropping to his stomach and hanging over the side.

My stomach rolled and my muscles strained as I shifted my son in my arms and then hoisted his limp upper body as high as I could. Tanner was able to catch him under the arms and pull him out of the water.

In any other situation, that would have meant safety.

But getting him out of the water was only the first hurdle we'd have to face.

As soon as he was out of my arms, Charlotte's caught my elbow. "Help me up!"

Her eyes were wild, but she didn't delay in using my body to climb on to the dock after him.

"Call nine-one-one!" Tanner screamed at everyone and no one as he moved out of Charlotte's way.

"Please. Please. Please. Let him be okay," I chanted to myself as I scrambled up, slicing my foot on a splintered edge of the wood. But the pain didn't even register among the agony in my chest.

Tanner moved to the side, and together, we helped our father up.

"Travis. Baby. Please!" Charlotte cried, tears dripping from her chin as she started chest compressions.

"What can I do?" I asked her, dropping beside them to my knees and brushing his dark-brown hair off his forehead.

"Move!" she barked before starting rescue breathing.

I lifted my hands in surrender and fell back onto my ass as my nightmare played out in front of me.

There was a bustle of activity around us. But my eyes never left Travis.

I aged at least fifty years as I watched her fevered efforts to revive our son, but nothing seemed to be working. And, as the seconds turned into minutes, I became more and more panicked that they never would.

I couldn't be sure how long it had been since he'd collapsed, but a surge of adrenaline and relief slammed into me when the paramedics finally appeared.

Charlotte rose off his body—and it killed me to admit it, but that was all it was at that point. She started rambling off orders and stats. Even as tears streamed from her eyes, she was able to list his medications and all of his health information.

Meanwhile, I could barely think.

My body was numb, and the air around us felt too thick to breathe.

I'd just gotten him back. We were supposed to be a family. Together. Forever.

This wasn't allowed to happen. There had been only one option with his heart condition, and dying was not it.

We were happy.

We were supposed to *stay* happy.

With hollow eyes and an equally hollow chest, I watched them load him onto a gurney, and then he was gone. Charlotte jogged beside him.

But I was stuck. Physically unable to move.

I blinked at the ground. The chair he had sat in only minutes earlier had been shoved out of the way, his fishing pole lost in the pond and his tackle box spilled out, various lures and hooks scattered around. But it was the wet silhouette of his body that tore my heart from my chest.

What if that was all that was left of him?

The sun still hung bright in the sky, but midnight fell all the same. And, in that moment, I feared I'd never escape it again.

The darkness was going to be my executioner.

It was going to crush me, suffocate me, and then devour me.

"Porter," someone called.

I snapped out of it long enough to see that it was Charlotte.

Hooking her arm in the air, she yelled, "Let's go! He needs you!"

Needs was present tense.

Hope roared to life inside me.

And only then did my feet become unstuck.

SIXTEEN

Charlotte

H E WAS ALIVE.

In bad shape.

But alive.

Which, as I was giving him CPR on my hands and knees, was more than I had thought possible.

After several failed attempts on the ambulance ride over, the ER doctors had been able to shock his weak heart back into a rhythm. Not since I had been pregnant, having my first ultrasound, had the sound of a heartbeat been so beautiful. But the minute the beeps of my son's heart rising and falling rang through the air as I stood helplessly outside the room, I collapsed to my knees.

I burst into tears and sank to the floor, Porter right beside me, his chest heaving in time with mine, a million curse words mixed with blessed praises rolling from our tongues.

We didn't touch. Or speak.

We didn't need words. Or comfort.

We needed a miracle.

The world moved in a flurry as I frantically tried to keep up, all the while watching my hopes and dreams fade out of reach.

We sat there for God only knows how long as doctors and nurses continued trying to stabilize him enough to move him to a room.

The hospital was a small community. And, once word had gotten around that my son had been admitted, the staff flooded the ER. Greg, my partner at North Point Pulmonology, was one of the first to arrive. He'd been acting as Travis's pulmonologist for the last few weeks, but his orders were coming from friends of mine at Texas Children's Hospital.

"Did you call them?" I asked, jumping to my feet.

Porter rose to his feet beside me and attempted to take my hand, but I shook it off.

"Did you?" I asked again.

Greg's concerned gaze dipped to my soaking-wet shirt and then back to my eyes. "I did. Erin said she can't get away, but Gina is catching a flight out." He lifted a finger at a passing nurse. "Can you grab them some scrubs to put on?"

"Listen. No. Call her back. We don't need a pulmonologist. I need a team of cardiologists. The best they have."

Porter moved into my side and added, "Dr. Kreh is the head of cardiology at TCH. I talked to him a few weeks ago on the phone. He's familiar with Travis's case."

Greg looked at him for only a beat and then ignored him altogether. His face became soft, and his words were gentle. "Charlotte, you know there is nothing he can do at this point."

"That's not true," I hissed.

He sighed and shoved his hands into his pockets. "You're thinking like a parent. Think like a doctor. There is no quick fix or treatment here. The muscles in his heart are no longer able to support his body. You've known this day was coming since he was born."

"I've had him back for two weeks!" My voice cracked. "It's not supposed to happen yet."

Greg cut his gaze to the floor, and Porter once again tried to pull me into his arms, but I refused him the contact.

I didn't want to be coddled. I wanted someone to make this stop.

To change the inevitable.

To fix my son.

"Make the call," I demanded.

"Charlotte, I—"

"Make the fucking call, Greg!" I boomed, getting in his face. "Do it!"

"I already did. He said there was nothing that he could do." He kept his eyes down. "He needs the transplant, Charlotte. I know this is hard for you. But we're going to find him a heart. I swear to you. This entire hospital has your back."

My body sagged, and the jagged knife of reality stabbed me in the gut. Medically, I knew that what he was saying was right. But, as a mom, I couldn't stop hoping that he was wrong.

"He's been on the list for two months," Porter said, "and we haven't gotten so much as a phone call."

"He'll be moved up the list," I whispered.

He glanced between Greg and me. "Okay. That's good, then, right?"

"Up doesn't mean the top."

"It's still *up*," Porter argued, the saddest tinge of hope coloring his voice.

I didn't carry the same hope. Lifting my pleading gaze to Greg, I asked, "He's not leaving this hospital, is he?"

His face paled, he closed his eyes, and then crushed me. "Not with that heart."

A wave of devastation slammed into me.

Four words.

Every single one of them broke me.

Slapping my hand over my mouth, I stumbled back a step.

With a hand at the back of my neck, Porter forced me against his chest and hugged me tight.

And, for the first time ever, I felt no comfort in his arms.

No warmth.

No solace.

I felt nothing but an ice-cold chill travel up my spine.

I stood there, desperately searching for the relief Porter usually gave me. My heart racing, my mouth dry. But nothing came to me. Not even when I closed my eyes and gave the darkness a try.

There was no reprieve to be found in a situation like that.

"Charlotte," someone called from down the hall.

My head popped up and I saw Brady racing through the ER, his terrified gaze morphing into a living, breathing beast as he came to a sudden stop several feet away. His wide eyes locked on Porter.

"Are you fucking kidding me?" he seethed.

I stepped out of Porter's arms and lifted my hands in surrender. "Don't start this here."

169

Porter stepped forward and rumbled, "We have bigger things to worry about than your bullshit right now, Brady." He moved behind me, snaking an arm around my hips and bringing his chest flush with my back.

With his callused gaze, Brady followed the motion down. "You cannot be serious. Why are you here right now?"

"We were together when Travis collapsed." I tried to explain.

He barked a laugh and planted his hands on his hips. "And why the fuck were you together, Charlotte? Please, God, tell me you aren't back together with the man who kidnapped your son. For fuck's sake, what is wrong with you?"

"He has a right to be here."

"He has no right!" Brady exploded.

Porter charged forward and he did it so fast that I didn't have a chance to stop him until it was too late. He grabbed Brady's throat and slammed his back into the wall. "I have every fucking right! That is my son. *Mine!*"

Brady's eyes bulged and his face turned red.

"Porter, let him go!" I clawed at his arm, but it was useless. Porter had a death grip on his neck.

"I have done *everything* for that child," Porter growled. "I was the one who held him each night when he cried through countless breathing treatments. I was the one who made sure he had the best medical care. I was the one who held his hand every time he was poked and prodded with needle after needle. And, not a goddamn hour ago, I dragged his lifeless body out of the water for a *second* time." He leaned in close until they were nose to nose. "I don't give a single damn what you or any court in this country says. He. Is. Mine!"

Just as quickly as Porter had grabbed Brady, he released him. Thrusting a hand into the top of his hair, he started to pace.

Brady hunched over and supported himself on his knees, coughing and cursing.

Two uniformed hospital security guards came barreling around the corner, their gazes bouncing between the two men.

"I'm sorry about that," I told the guards. "We have this completely under control now."

"Arrest...him." Brady wheezed, flinging a hand out at Porter.

"Brady, no!" I yelled.

He straightened to his full height and rolled his shoulders back. "We have a protection order against that man. I want him out of here now!"

"You selfish coward," Porter snarled.

I stepped in front of the officers. "Please. Stop. Just listen—"

"Is this true?" the younger of the two men asked.

I glared at Brady. "Please don't do this... Travis's condition is bad, Brady. Like, we don't know if he'll ever walk out of this hospital again. If he wakes up and wants to see his dad—"

"Then I'll be here," Brady snapped.

Porter exploded all over again, and the guards quickly intervened, grabbing his arms to hold him back.

"You son of a bitch!" Porter shouted. "You can't stand the idea that he needs me."

Brady's lips curled menacingly. "He doesn't need you. He *wants* you because he doesn't know any better. Six months from now, he won't even remember you exist."

"Brady!" I hissed.

He swung his malevolent gaze my way. "And *you*. Whenever the fuck your boyfriend there gets out of jail, you can have him all to yourself. Because, *when* our son comes home, it's going to be to *my* house. I am done playing this shit your way. You fucking lost him the first time. I shouldn't even have trusted him with you this long."

My mouth fell open as my whole body went up in flames.

"You piece of shit!" Porter roared, and then his voice faded away as I heard a scuffle behind me.

But I didn't tear my gaze off the biological father of my son long enough to see where they were taking his real father.

With calculated steps, I prowled toward Brady.

With every blink came darkness and light.

And with every heartbeat came a reminder of death and life.

Stopping in front of him, I stared up at him and stated, calm and cool, "I know you hate me for what happened all those years ago. And there hasn't been a minute over the last decade where I didn't wish I could change it. But no matter what you say. And no matter how hard you try. I will *always* be his mother."

"And I will always be his father."

"No. Brady. You are the selfish man who showed up at the hospital after getting a phone call that your *son* had been rushed to the emergency room completely unresponsive and you haven't asked about him once. Porter was there when he needed a father today. And Porter has been there for him when he needed a father every day since he adopted him seven years ago. If you were any kind of man at all, you would drop to your knees and thank him for giving our son a beautiful life. Instead, you're slinging insults and having him arrested while our son is not twenty feet away, fighting for his life."

I took a step closer and moved my lips to his ears. "This is *your* only warning. You need to prepare yourself for the world of hurt I'm going to rain down over you if you so much as think of taking my son away from me. I will spare no expense to make it happen. I will cut you deeper than your shallow soul knew possible. Because. Brady. You're right. I did lose him. But make no mistake about it. Nothing. No one. Not you. And not even the face of death will ever take my son away from me again."

Stepping away, I gave him my back, a new resolve coursing through my veins, making me stronger than I had ever been before.

"You're a fucking joke, Charlotte," he called. "You'll be lucky to get visitation after this shit."

Any other day, his *words* would have destroyed me.

But, right then, I had bigger things to worry about than Brady throwing yet another hissy fit.

First being to escort my son up to Pediatric ICU and discuss his current state with his cardiologists.

Second being to contact my attorney and give her a heads-up on Brady's latest threats.

Third being to get Porter out of jail.

And last being to suck in a deep breath and remind myself that I had too many reasons to live to shut down again— no matter how hard it got.

Two hours later...

"Get him out of there, Tom."

"Charlotte, honey. It's not that easy."

After pulling the sweater my mother had brought me tight around my shoulders, I crossed my arms and began to pace up and down the hospital hallway. "Then make it that easy."

He shoved his hands into his pockets and stared at the floor. "I'm sorry, but I can't in good conscience help Porter Reese."

I stopped and leveled my gaze on his. "Then you have no business here. Feel free to leave."

"*You* are my business," he clipped. "And you're not making smart choices."

I marched over to him, and then, careful to keep my voice low, I seethed, "I was never your business. You got assigned to a case of a missing baby." I stabbed a finger at Travis's hospital room. "That means that little boy is your business. So, by all means, walk your ass in there and tell him you aren't going to help his father get out of jail because you feel like maybe, just maybe, Porter outsmarted you at some point."

He glared at me. "That is not what this is about. This is about you being so blinded by your heart that you can't even see the truth."

"You're right!" I whispered. "I am blinded by love." I planted my hands on my hips and leaned in close. "Love for my son. When he wakes up and Porter isn't standing at that bedside, it's going to crush him. And there is nothing I won't do to prevent him from feeling even an ounce of heartbreak."

He cocked his head to the side. "And what about you?

You love Porter?"

Defiantly, I held his stare. "Unquestionably."

He clamped his jaw shut and ground his teeth. "You're just going to forget that that man raised your son for the last however many years? That he married the sociopath who stole him? That he pursued you knowing he had your son? He played you then. And, now, he's playing you again to keep that boy in his life. I don't doubt that he loves that little boy. But I refuse to stand by and watch him treat you like a pawn in this little game of his."

"He didn't know he had my son!"

"Yeah," he scoffed. "So he's said a million times."

"You found nothing on him. The investigation has been closed."

"Because we can't get enough on the asshole to make a case. But that doesn't mean he's not guilty. Coincidences like that don't just happen, Charlotte. For fuck's sake, he was at your house the day the body of the real Travis Reese was recovered."

"Travis Hendrix," I corrected.

"What?" he clipped.

"That little boy whose body you recovered. His name was Travis Hendrix. And he died years before Porter ever entered the equation. You want to talk about games and pawns. Shit, Tom. Porter was caught in the middle of the ultimate chess match and he didn't even know he was playing. Can we all take a step back and point the finger where blame really belongs? Catherine took my son."

"I know that," he grumbled.

"Can we also acknowledge that she had some pretty serious mental health issues?"

"No one is doubting that."

"Then can you imagine how in the hell my son's life would have turned out if Porter had not been in that picture?"

His eyebrows knit together as he cut his gaze away.

I inched closer and rested my hands on his chest. "Yeah, Tom. He'd be dead and you know it. The first time she got overwhelmed with his health and Porter hadn't been there to talk her off the ledge, she'd have taken his life right then so she wouldn't have to lose him again."

"Jesus, Charlotte," he whispered. "That doesn't make what he's doing to you okay."

"What he's doing to me?" I asked. "Let me tell you exactly what he's doing to me, Tom. He's making me happy. He's making me laugh. And, even when I'm crying, he makes me feel safe. He makes me feel loved. He's reminding me that the world is full of light even when you can't see it. And, more than all of that, he's shown me that there doesn't have to be light for something to be beautiful. Love can grow in the darkness, Tom. I know this is true because of him."

At the thought, Porter's warmth enveloped me. He didn't even have to be in the room to soothe me.

Tom rested his hand on my hip and gave me a squeeze. "Charlotte—"

"I'm going to let you off the hook here. I know you think Porter is playing me. And, being the big tough detective-slash-father-figure, nothing I say is going to change your mind. But let me tell you this: If the way I feel with Porter is the product of a game, then I am willing to be his pawn for the rest of my life." I sucked in a shaky breath. "He makes me happy, Tom. Remember that woman at the restaurant you and

Mom saw a while back? The one whose face was bright and her laugh was loud?"

His face became impossibly gentle, and he swallowed as he nodded.

I stared deep into his eyes, begging for him to believe me. "He makes me that woman."

He sighed, and his strong shoulders rounded with defeat. "For the record, I'm not okay with this." He looked up, his eyes blazing with love. "But there isn't one damn thing in this world I wouldn't do to make you happy."

I grinned in victory. "Including getting Porter out of jail?"

SEVENTEEN

Porter

I WAS FALLING APART, PACING IN THAT HOLDING CELL. IT WAS nine the next morning and I still hadn't been able to so much as call someone. The stench of piss and vomit from the guy asleep on the bench beside me was enough to melt my nose hairs, but that wasn't why I was sick to my stomach. I had no idea how Travis was doing, where Hannah was, or how Charlotte was holding up. I had too many people depending on me to be stuck behind bars because of a worthless order of protection.

I'd asked for my lawyer no less than seven thousand times, but if anyone had heard, no one was acting on it. I was losing my patience. Well, what was left of it, anyway.

Brady Boyd had caught the brunt of me losing it. And, if it hadn't been for the security guards, he would have been on the receiving end of me losing *all* of it. I hadn't known that it was possible to hate that motherfucker more than I already did. Oh, but the minute he'd opened his mouth to Charlotte, a whole new level of loathing usually reserved for Catherine had opened up inside me. And the day's emotional upheaval had manifested in rage. I'd have felt bad if the asshole didn't deserve it. But, when he'd mentioned taking Travis away from Charlotte, I had known he deserved a whole hell of a lot worse than I'd ever dole out.

"Hey!" I yelled at an officer as he passed by my cell. "Any word on my attorney?"

"Yeah, I got word," a quasi-familiar voice replied from the other end of the hallway.

I strained my head against the bars, hope spiraling inside me only for it to fall flat as Tom Stafford came marching toward me.

"Son of a bitch," I mumbled under my breath.

According to Charlotte, Tom was not one of my biggest fans. According to every run-in I'd ever had with the man since the truth about Travis had come out, he hated me with a fucking passion. Either way, his being there was not a good sign.

"Not a single word," he ordered when he stopped in front of me.

I held his stoic gaze as he motioned for one of the uniforms to unlock the cell door.

I sent up a million thanks to whomever had brainwashed him into releasing me.

They seemed a tad premature the minute he caught my arm and started dragging me down the hall.

Without the first fucking clue of where he was taking me or if I was even being released, I couldn't help myself. He was

179

my only lifeline to my son.

"How's Travis?" I asked.

"Shut it, Porter," he growled.

"You have to give me something. I've been wearing holes in the floor, stuck in this godforsaken place all night."

"Shut. Up." He jerked my arm as two police officers turned the corner and came strolling toward us.

They all shared chin jerks.

I momentarily quieted as they passed.

And then I dove right back into my questions. "What about Charlotte? How's she holding up?"

He suddenly stopped and shoved me against a wall. "For once, do what you are goddamn told and shut your fucking mouth."

"Is that what you would do in my situation?" I shot back. "Shut your mouth while the people you love are falling to pieces around you? Fuck that, Tom. I am *not* that man."

He turned his eyes to the ceiling and mumbled, "I did not sign up for this bullshit."

"And you think I did? You think I willingly signed up to have my whole life flipped upside down? My child snatched from me? My woman's heart broken time and fucking time again? This is my nightmare. I know you hate it, but Charlotte is my family. And I'm not quitting my family. No matter how hard you and Brady try to fight me. You can lock me up, throw away the key, but I will never stop trying to keep my family together."

"For fuck's sake, son. Give it a rest." He grabbed my arm again and started dragging me toward a mystery door at the end of the hallway.

"I want to talk to my attorney," I demanded.

"And you will get that a hell of a lot quicker if you shut your mouth."

I silently followed him for a few more steps before adding, "I'm serious, Tom. I love her. Charlotte and those kids are my life."

"Jesus Christ," he cussed, stopping at the door. "I got it, okay? You love Charlotte. She loves you. The world is filled with rainbows and butterflies when you two are together… yadda yadda yadda." He snatched the door open and shoved me through it. "Listen to your attorney this time, son."

"Porter!" Charlotte called as I stumbled into the waiting room at the front of the police station.

I blinked. Tanner was there, huddled together with…

I blinked again. My two attorneys?

I had no fucking idea how the tide had turned and I was now a free man, but I wasn't about to waste time asking questions—at least, not about that.

I moved straight to Charlotte. "How's Travis?"

She grinned and a blast of relief filled my empty chest. "Hanging in there. He's still on the vent, but Greg and the cardiologist agree, so they're going to wean him off it today. I want to be there for that, so I gave Brady some time with him this morning."

My jaw turned hard, and I could only imagine the fury on my face.

She pressed up onto her toes and brushed her lips with mine. "Relax. My mom is up there too. She knows to call me if anything changes. I don't have a choice but to let him see him. However, we do have a choice how we handle this from here on out."

"And how exactly is that?" I asked, sour settling in my mouth.

"You're going to have to stay away from the hospital until our court date."

My blood ignited into a vicious inferno. "No fucking way."

She rested her hands on my chest. "Listen, Porter. Tom and your attorneys spoke with Judge Gratham to get you released. They told him about Travis's heart and that, when he collapsed, it was a highly emotional situation, but they have assured him that you breaking the order was a one-time thing."

My eyebrows shot up. "We've been basically living together for a week."

She cut her gaze away, and her cheeks pinked. "Yeah… We, um…decided to leave that part out."

"How? We were at Tanner's for a cookout when the ambulance picked him up."

"Uh, no. *We* were not anywhere. Travis and I stopped by Tanner's to pick up some more of his things. You just happened to show up about the time Travis collapsed."

I closed my eyes—that sour in my stomach turning into rot. "So, we're flat-out lying to the police now?"

She looped her arms around my hips and shifted closer. "Porter, we're doing what we have to do to stay together and keep you out of jail. It's not ideal. But it worked. Judge Gratham signed off on your release and agreed to move up our court date to two days from now so that you can hopefully be allowed supervised visitation while Travis is in the hospital."

"Supervised visitation. Outstanding."

"*I'll* be supervising it. So, really, it will be like any other night that we are all together. Isn't that what matters? That we're all together?"

I groaned. "It's not sexy when you use my words against me."

She smiled and it soothed the worry inside me. "Well, good. Because there is nothing sexy about the way you smell right now." She giggled and tried to push me away, but I held her close

"Excuse me. I stepped out of the county jail, not a day spa."

Still wearing a gorgeous smile, she peered up at me through her lashes. "We're going to be okay, Porter."

"I know. I'm just sick of all the bullshit."

"We'll video chat, okay? The minute he comes around, I'll call you and Hannah and we'll hang out like that for the next few days."

I nodded even though my heart was screaming for me to say fuck it all and head straight up to that hospital to see my son. But, if I wanted any hope of us being together again, I had to play by the rules.

I kissed her forehead. "What'd you have to do to get Tom in on this?"

"I batted my eyelashes and cried a little. He was no match for my guilt trip."

I barked a laugh. "I'm not sure if I should be proud of you or worried about our future together now."

She curled in close. "Worried, probably."

I touched my lips to the top of her head. "One of these days, our lives will become boring. We're going to be sitting on a couch together, asking each other repeatedly, 'What's for dinner?' and getting frustrated when we come up with no answers. The kids are going to be wandering around, complaining, and whining that they have nothing to do. There will be nothing on TV. No good movies out. The weather will be crappy and the four of us will be stuck in the house all damn day, fighting and bickering with each other for no other reason than it provides two minutes of excitement. And I swear to you. That will be the happiest day of my entire life. This shit, where every day is another drama, is killing me."

She craned her head back and dreamily stared up at me. "That sounds amazing."

Just then, Tanner came strolling over. "How many times am I going to have to bail you out of jail?"

I smirked. "Now you know how I felt when we were in college."

"Touché," he replied.

Charlotte rolled her eyes and then looked up at me. "I have to get back to the hospital. I don't want him waking up without me."

I groaned, my heart aching at the thought of not being there when he needed me the most. But it eased me to know that at least Charlotte would be there. "Yeah. Definitely. Get up there."

"I love you, Porter. Just a few more days."

"I love you too. Take care of my boy."

"Hey, buddy!" I cooed in a baby voice I knew for a fact he hated, but I couldn't bring myself to care. I was seeing my son alive and awake for the first time since I'd dragged him out of that pond.

I hated that it was via a damn video chat, but beggars can't be choosers. And, right then, I was a beggar to the highest power. It had been a horrible twenty-four hours. At that time just the day before, we had been laughing and eating pasta salad. Now, my son was covered in wires and laid up in a hospital bed, waiting for a heart that may or may not come.

"Hey, Dad," he said weakly.

He looked like hell—dark circles under his eyes, his face swollen and still pale. But his heart was beating, and that was all that mattered.

"Let me see him!" Hannah yelled, climbing up onto my bed and into my lap. "Hey, Travis."

"Hey, Hannie," he mumbled.

"How ya doing?" I asked, turning the phone on the side so he could see both Hannah and me in the same frame.

"Not good," he groaned.

My stomach pitched, but Charlotte immediately moved the phone to her face and corrected him.

"He's doing great. His BP is steady, pulse ox is coming up, and his EKG looks better than any of us had hoped. He's still a little groggy and tired from the medication, but as soon as that wears off, he should start feeling better."

"Okay. Good," I whispered when I didn't trust my voice.

God, this sucked. In all of the times Travis had gone to the hospital, I'd always been the one to go with him. And, now, I was stuck at home like some kind of caged animal waiting for permission to see my own damn son.

"And, now, he's asleep," Charlotte drawled, flashing the camera to my son, his eyes closed and his mouth hanging open in slumber.

I chuckled at the sight, but it did nothing to tame the anger brewing inside me.

"Go watch your movie, baby," I told Hannah. "I'm going to talk to Charlotte for a minute and then I'll be out."

"Okay," she chirped. "Bye, Charlotte."

"Goodnight, Hannah. I'll see you soon."

Hannah started to climb off the bed, but then she froze and leaned back into the frame. "Travis only likes red and orange Jell-O. If he gets green, Daddy brings it home to me."

Charlotte laughed. "I'll be sure to set it aside for you."

Hannah nodded and then wandered out of the room.

I shoved two pillows behind me and reclined against the headboard. Once I was settled, I asked, "How are you holding up?"

She quietly moved through the hospital room and into the bathroom, where she shut the door. "I'm okay, actually. He really is looking better, Porter."

"Like, good enough to maybe come home?" Even I heard the hope in my voice.

She winced and shook her head.

"Right. Of course," I said, pretending like I hadn't been stabbed in the gut.

"He's going to get a heart, Porter. I can feel it."

"I'm glad you can, because I'm not feeling anything these days but a whole lot of worry and dread," I replied, swinging my legs over the side of the bed. But I found myself unable to get comfortable.

"Turn off the light, Porter," she whispered.

I shook my head. "I can't. I need to go feed Hannah dinner.

Something with, like, an actual vegetable. Mom dropped her off earlier and I swear she had a lollipop stuck in her hair. I love my mom, but she takes the job of spoiling her grandkids seriously."

She stared at me blankly. "Off, Porter."

"It's still daylight outside, Charlotte. I could turn all the lights in the house off and it wouldn't never be dark enough."

"Okay. You want to talk in the light?"

Suddenly, a lump of emotion lodged in my throat and I had to force the words around it. "Is this the light? Because it sure as hell doesn't feel like it."

"Everything is going to be okay. He's asleep, baby. I feel really good about his stats—as a mother *and* a doctor."

I shook my head. "See…that's the problem. I felt really good yesterday. I was lecturing you on holding on to the happy times and not allowing the fears to consume you. And here I am, learning that it was a bunch of bullshit. Just because you don't think about the future doesn't mean it won't one day become the present. I've known this day was coming for a long time with Travis. And I still feel like it came out of nowhere." I turned my face away from the phone with hopes that she didn't see me wiping my cheek on my shoulder.

Fuck. I was supposed to be the man here. I should have been the one taking care of my family. My woman. My son. Protecting them from the harsh realities of life.

And there I was, helpless and grounded like a fucking teenager who'd stayed out past his curfew.

I cleared my throat, but that pain-filled lump settled right back in. "And this waiting bullshit? That's all I've been doing recently. Waiting on custody hearings. Waiting on the cops to clear my name. Waiting for the judge to allow me supervised visitation. And, now, I have to wait on someone to die so my child can get a goddamn heart? I mean, what the fuck am I supposed to do with that?"

She bit her bottom lip. "I don't know. But I'm doing the exact same thing."

"Swear to God, Charlotte. Tanner and I passed a fucking fender bender on the way home and my first thought was, oh maybe someone died. Who does that?"

"Desperate parents do that, baby. All the time. You aren't alone in that guilt."

My heart thundered in my ears as I confessed, "But that's the thing. I don't even feel guilty." I rose from the bed and began pacing, holding the phone out in front of me even though I wished I could hurl it across the room.

"And you aren't alone in that, either."

"I feel like I'm losing my mind."

"And you're entitled to that. It's been a tough two weeks for all of us. But the key words here are *two weeks*. A few weeks ago, I didn't think I'd last a day in this hell. But we've made it through two weeks. And, now, we're going to make it through the next two days. And then, together, with Travis and Hannah, we're going to make it through the next however long it takes for him to get a heart. We can do this, Porter. And we *will* do this—because there is no other choice."

I stopped pacing and allowed her words to infuse me. There had been a lot of days in my life, not just over the last two weeks, when I'd thought the world was going to swallow me. After Catherine died, I hadn't had the first clue how I'd ever move past that kind of hurt and betrayal. But I had. And, through that, I'd found Charlotte.

The day I'd met her, I'd told myself that people entered our lives for a reason, and I was determined to figure out why she had come into mine. Logic told me it was because I'd needed her to treat my son. The more spiritual answer was that I was raising her son and the heavens saw it fit for us to figure that out. But, right then, as I stared at her on the phone, her brown eyes bright with love and her face strong and fearless, I decided that this was the reason she'd come into mine.

Without her, I'd still be lost in the hate and pain.

Without her, this would have been another source to feed the constant rage forever growing inside me.

Today would have come regardless if I'd met her or not. Travis had been fated to need that heart from the get-go. But Charlotte quieted my storm. She extinguished the fire. And she soothed my demons.

Without her, I'd be lost in darkness. Alone.

Sinking to the bed, I closed my eyes and willed my pulse to slow.

She stayed silent, in true Charlotte fashion, until I was ready to return to the world of rational thinking.

"Hi," I whispered as I lifted my lids.

"Hi," she whispered back.

"You stole my line with that whole 'no other choice' bit," I told her, my smile tight.

"Then take it back," she told me. Her gorgeous grin felt like a drowning man's first breath of air.

"There's no other choice. He's going to be okay."

"And..." she prompted.

"And..." I drawled in question.

"And we're going to stick together before, during, and after it happens."

I fell back on the bed, holding her smiling face above me. "Well, that was a given. You are stuck with me for the rest of your life."

"Good," she smarted. "Ian will be happy to have the company."

I barked a laugh. "Did I forget to mention that I swung by your place on my way home?"

"Porter," she warned.

"Yeeeaaaaah. I hate to be the one to break this to you, but there was an accident involving Ian."

She laughed. "Porter, I swear I will hunt you down."

"It seems he tripped into the shredder."

"You are such a liar. One, I don't have a shredder. And two, he's, like, six feet tall and made of cardboard. No way he's going to fit in a shredder."

God, I loved this with her. Even stupid shit about her Ian Somerhalder cardboard cutout made me smile wider than I'd ever thought possible. It was fun and it was light, not at all like the suffocating shroud that cloaked us on a daily basis. But it was moments like that, when we got to be just two people in love, that gave me the strength to carry on for another day.

"You'd be amazed how affordable an industrial shredder is on Amazon."

"Porter!" she scolded and then burst into quiet laughter.

That sound alone was more than enough to get me through the next two days.

EIGHTEEN

Charlotte

"Hey, baby," I whispered before kissing Porter long and deep.

"Mmmm," he groaned into my mouth as his strong arms held me against his chest. "God, I missed you."

"It's only been two days," I taunted. Though, not-so-secretly considering I'd all but mounted him the moment he'd gotten out of his car; I'd missed him too.

He set me back on my feet and then straightened his navy-blue suit coat. "Two days too long. How's Trav this morning?"

"He's..." *Getting worse.*

When I'd left that morning, his cardiologist wouldn't even look me in the eye. It was literally overnight that he had gone from winning the uphill climb to crashing back down to below baseline. His decreased heart function was taking its toll on his lungs and liver to the point that I worried that, even if a heart did arrive, he wouldn't be physically strong enough to handle the stress of the surgery. I hadn't slept in what felt like forever because all I could do was stay awake, night after night, and watch his vitals.

Swallowing hard, I finished on a semi-lie "He's doing fine. Mom and Tom are with him."

Porter nodded, but judging by the purse of his lips, he wasn't buying it. He could see right through me. However, he didn't want to acknowledge the hovering reality any more than I did.

We weren't exactly pretending as much as faking positivity.

"As soon as we finish here, we'll go straight up to the hospital," I whispered.

He shot me a genuine smile, one of the first I'd seen from him in a while. "Yeah. I can't wait to see him."

Hand in hand, we walked up the courthouse steps. Once we'd gotten through the metal detectors, we found our attorneys huddled together in quiet conversation.

"Hey, Mark," Porter said.

Mark's gaze cut to me and then dipped to Porter's hand in mine. "So, this is the front we're portraying?"

Porter's forehead crinkled. "This is the only front I have. So, yeah, this is what we're portraying."

Mark stared at us for a beat longer like he had something to say that wouldn't quite come out.

My attorney, Victoria, moved to my side, her shoulder brushing with mine as she whispered, "You sure about this guy?"

I hooked a finger at Porter. "Him? No. I just found him in the parking lot."

Her lips thinned as she cut her gaze to Mark. "Charlotte, as I told you, Brady has filed for *full* custody. This is not something to joke around with. After the scuffle at the hospital and Porter breaking the order of protection, being here with him is not going to help your case. And, quite honestly, if you lose custody, it's not going to help Porter, either."

A hum of adrenaline started in my fingertips before clawing its way through my body. "I'm *not* losing custody. I have done nothing wrong. Porter has been cleared of all involvement in the kidnapping. We were dating before we knew about Travis. And we're dating after. This should be a non-issue. And if this *is* an issue, I'm paying you an exorbitant amount of money to *make* it a non-issue."

Porter's hand tensed around mine in silent agreement.

"Relax," she urged. "We're on the same team."

"Right. So, please"—I pointedly looked to Mark and then back to Victoria—"act like it."

Side-glances were exchanged between the two of them, but they eventually nodded and stepped away.

I huffed and chanced a glance up at Porter, fully expecting a scowl to be covering his handsome face.

It wasn't.

A sexy-as-sin smirk pulled at his lips. "You are so getting laid tonight," he whispered. "That whole 'make it a non-issue' thing was hot."

I rolled my eyes, but only to hide the fact that my stomach was fluttering. "It's true though. Combined, we could probably put Travis through college for what this is costing us. And, paying this kind of money, I sure as hell don't expect it to come with a heaping side of judgment."

He grinned again and bent low to kiss me. "I like the idea of us putting Travis through college together."

My whole body warmed as I stared into his blue eyes. "I like the idea of that, too."

"All right. Break it up, you two," Tanner said, sidling up beside his brother.

"Where's Dad?" Porter asked.

"At home, probably digging cash out of his mattress for bail money."

Porter's eyebrows shot up. "For which one of us?"

Tanner straightened his ridiculous pink-and-white-striped tie, which only he could make look masculine. "If he's smart? Both."

Porter grinned. Tanner's lips split to match.

Tanner leaned around his brother and aimed that mega-watt moneymaker on me. "I owe you big time."

"For what?"

"For that." He jutted his chin down the hall.

I turned and found Rita clipping toward us in a fitted black dress and a red pair of stilettos.

"Don't even pretend that you didn't have something to do with her showing up at my door last night," he said.

"Oh, I had *everything* to do with that, Sloth. And don't worry. I'll let you know when I think of some way for you to return the favor. But, in the meantime"—I lowered my voice to a whisper—"don't show your ass in here today and make me regret it. I don't care what Brady says. You keep your mouth shut."

He lifted his hand to his temple in a salute and clicked out of the corner of his mouth. "Aye aye, captain." His gaze heated as he slid it to Rita. "Hey there, my sexy lady," he greeted in a sultry bedroom purr that I feared could impregnate her from across the room.

He frowned when my best friend came to me first.

"Hey, honey. You nervous?"

"Not really," I answered. "I just want to get this over with so can we go back up to the hospital and be with Travis."

"Good. Because it's going to be great." She reached into her black Fendi satchel and pulled a stack of papers out. "This is everything you asked for. Including a few more that I dug up on my own." She winked. "You got this."

I took the papers from her hand. "Thank you. You have no idea how much I appreciate this."

She gave my arm a squeeze and then clipped her way around to Tanner, muttering, "Okay. Okay. Hold your horses. I'm coming. Jeesh, you Reese men sure are needy."

Tanner wrapped her into a bear hug, and she started giggling as he murmured something in her ear.

I smiled on the inside, enjoying the idea that people we loved were finally happy too.

"What's that?" Porter asked, tilting his head to the papers in my hand.

"You'll see in a little while."

He smirked. "Naked pictures?"

I purposefully kept my face blank as I replied, "Yeah. Of Tanner."

He narrowed his eyes. "For the record, I find you negative amounts of funny right now."

"For the record, I find you negative amounts of funny most of the time. But I love you anyway."

He chuckled and opened his mouth to reply, but he didn't get the words out.

"Incoming," Tanner whispered.

We all turned and saw Brady and his wife striding toward us, his angry, green gaze leveled on me.

Porter rolled his shoulders back and straightened so he stood a little taller, his muscles flexing under the confines of his suit.

"Ignore him," I said, leaning into my man's side.

Porter grunted in acknowledgment, but he tracked Brady all the way until he disappeared into the courtroom.

"You two ready?" Mark asked, Victoria smoothing her skirt out beside him.

I looked up at Porter. "Are we ready?"

His eyes blazed with determination as he stared down at me. "Let's do this."

Together, we walked into the courtroom, our attorneys leading the way. The last time we'd been in that room, Porter and I had been on opposite sides. Now, it was Brady who sat across the aisle.

Tension was thick in the air, but Porter kept his hand firmly in mine as we were seated. After a few moments of waiting, Judge Gratham came in, his scrutinizing gaze sweeping through the room.

"Please be seated," he said, sinking into his chair. "Well, this is a different seating arrangement since the last time. Mr. Boyd, it seems you are at the wrong table."

Brady's attorney pushed to his feet. "No, your honor. My client has—"

"Yeah. Yeah. Yeah. Full custody. I read all the paperwork.

I'm interested in hearing from Mr. Boyd about this sudden change though."

Brady whispered something to his attorney and then rose to his feet. "I no longer feel that it is in Lucas's best interest to remain in Charlotte's care. She has continuously proven that she is unable to put her personal life aside and make objective decisions for his well-being. She knowingly put him in danger only a few days ago, which resulted in him collapsing into a pond, where he had to be resuscitated."

I blinked. There was no fucking way I'd heard him correctly.

Shooting to my feet, I asked, "Are you blaming me for him having a heart attack?"

The judge motioned for me to sit with two fingers, and Mark and Victoria both tried to pull me down. Porter didn't move. Not even an inch. His jaw was ticking and his eyes were aimed forward at the judge, an inferno brewing within.

"As I was saying," Brady continued. "Her continuous involvement with Mr. Reese has not only gone against the order of protection issued by this court, but it has also impaired my ability to develop a relationship with my son."

"And there it is." I laughed sardonically. "The real reason why we're here."

"Ms. Mills," the judge said, turning his icy glare on me. "Do not make me have you removed from this courtroom. You'll have a chance to speak in a minute."

I grumbled and lowered myself back into my chair.

Porter still hadn't moved.

Brady grinned victoriously. "Furthermore, Charlotte has yet to secure any kind of housing for our son. She is currently living in a one-bedroom apartment that is not suitable for a young boy. I have a home where he could have his own bedroom and plenty of space to move around. It just makes sense that he be placed with me. And, honestly, the only reason I didn't press this issue sooner is that Charlotte seemed unstable when we first got Lucas back and I feared for our son's safety if I pushed her over the edge."

My mouth fell open as I stared at him. Shock and surprise mingled in a heady combination with betrayal and anger. Brady and I weren't close by any stretch of the imagination, but this was a new all-time low for him.

"How do you sleep at night?" I whispered, the hurt thick in my tone.

Porter's hand dropped to my lap, but I was too wound up to play the hand holding game.

Brady's gaze flicked to mine and bounced away just as quickly.

Lifting my hand in the air like a grade school student, I asked, "May I please speak now, your honor?"

He motioned for Brady to sit. Then he leaned back in his chair, intertwined his fingers, and rested them on his round stomach. "By all means, Ms. Mills."

"My son, *Travis*"—I aimed a pointed scowl at Brady— "was born with a heart condition called dilated cardiomyopathy. In short, his heart is enlarged and cannot efficiently pump blood. Due to decreased heart function, this condition can affect other organs in the body. And, for our son, his lungs have struggled the most. Now, with that said, nothing I did or didn't do caused my son to collapse the other day. However, as a medical professional, I'm willing to wager that the stress of the last few weeks has taken its toll on his already frail body. So, if anyone wants to point the finger at why he is laid up in a hospital bed right now, slowly fading away while waiting for a new heart to become available, it would be aimed at every single person in this room in one way or another.

"And as far as Brady calling me unstable? I honestly don't know how to respond to that. It's not only insulting and un-true, but it's disgusting to me that he would even go there after the hell we've been through. The last few weeks have been an emotional hurricane for all of us, but Travis has always been my number-one priority. I've taken a leave of absence from work, and finding a new house is at the top of my list. Between these court dates, ensuring Travis is able to spend ample time with Brady, and my son's numerous doctors' appointments and, now, hospital visits, there hasn't been a lot of time left in the day. We are all still adjusting. I am no exception."

I swallowed hard and then sucked in a deep breath that did nothing to soothe the nerves tap-dancing in my stomach. "Now, I'm not here to discuss or defend my private relation-ship with Porter Reese. However, it is impossible to discuss my son without talking about him."

I lifted the stack of papers Rita had delivered. "This is over one hundred signed statements from people who have interacted with Travis and Porter over the years. You will find letters from doctors, nurses, teachers, babysitters, employees, former employees, therapists, neighbors." I paused to smile. "I think there might even be a grocery store clerk or two. But, regardless of who they are, they all say the exact same thing. Porter loves his children." My voice cracked under the heavy weight of that truth.

"Jesus," he breathed beside me, taking the papers from my hand and starting to flip through them.

"It took me less than two days to get all of those statements," I told the judge. "I think I only made maybe five calls, and then those five people made five more calls, and so on and so forth. It was the easiest thing I've ever done. People came out of the woodwork wanting to support Porter."

"Jesus," he repeated.

I cleared my throat. "So, back to why I'm telling you this. My son is amazing. He's happy. He's received top-notch medical treatment. Private tutors. And he even went to Disney World with his family a few years back." My chin quivered and I forced a grin to cover it. "I know this because he's told me about it no less than twelve dozen times." My nose stung as I admitted, "I wasn't there for any of those things. But that doesn't mean I'm not grateful they happened. It's hard not to be jealous that someone else was there for your child when he grew up." I turned to look at Brady, tears falling from my eyes. "I swear I get it. You want to be his dad. His *only* dad. But the reason you can't build a relationship with your son has nothing to do with Porter and everything to do with the fact that you're building it on a foundation of jealousy. Porter shouldn't even be in your equation."

Brady sheepishly looked away, so I turned my attention back to the judge.

"I guess what I'm saying is, of all the ways this horrible ordeal could have turned out, I'm just happy this is how it ended. Porter took exceptional care of our child when we were not there to do it. So, yeah, my relationship with him aside, he deserves to be in Travis's life." I sniffled and barely managed to choke out, "A child can never be loved by too many good people."

Porter suddenly rose to his feet, curled his hand around the back of my neck, and dragged me into his chest. "Jesus Christ. Stop talking."

The courtroom was silent as Porter held me tighter than ever before. His deep and raspy I-love-yous echoed in my ear. My body sagged in his arms, the comfort and warmth only he possessed quelling the storm inside me.

"Well, okay, then. Anything else from you, Mr. Boyd?" Judge Gratham asked at the same time my phone started vibrating in my pocket.

"Charlotte," Brady called with urgency.

I didn't have much else to say to the man. If he was ready for round two, I was going to have to sit it out.

Turning in Porter's arm, I groaned, "Please, just stop. I can't—"

"We got a heart," he whispered, lifting his phone in the air as if I could read the message on the screen.

Chills exploded over my skin. "What?"

Porter echoed me. "What?"

Brady's eyes bulged wide at the same time a giant smile split his face. "We got a heart!"

Time stopped.

I understood what he was saying, but it felt too incredible to be real. So I asked again, "What?"

Porter patted my pockets down before fishing my phone out. He let out a loud laugh that broke at the end as he announced, "They found him a heart."

"We gotta go!" Brady exclaimed, rushing toward the door,

only slowing long enough to take his wife's hand and drag her after him.

But I didn't move.

"Porter?" I whispered and tilted my head back to see him.

His pleading, blue gaze was locked at the judge. "Please, your honor. Let me see him before he goes into surgery. It could be the last time—"

"It's not going to be the last time," the judge said matter-of-factly. "But go ahead, son. Get out of here. All of you. Supervised visitation is granted. Your attorneys and I will work out the visitation details until I can make a final ruling on custody."

My chest swelled.

Porter's breath left him on a rush. "Oh God. Thank you so much."

"I don't want to hear one word about you and Mr. Boyd getting into any more hospital brawls."

"No, sir. Of course not."

He smiled and made a shooing motion with his hands. "Good luck today. I'll be praying for your boy."

"Thank you," Porter and I called in unison as we raced from the room.

Hand in hand.

Together.

NINETEEN

Porter

"I LOVE YOU," I WHISPERED TO MY SON AS WE SURROUNDED him in the pre-op room.

"I love you too," he slurred, a goofy smile on his face.

The nurse had just slipped a little something into his IV to relax him while we waited for an anesthesiologist to show up.

Charlotte was standing beside me, looking over his chart for what had to be the tenth time, and Brady was glaring at me from the corner.

I hated that man something fierce. I could have overlooked it if he had been an ass just to me. But he'd been giving Charlotte hell for over a decade, blaming her for what Catherine had done. It took every good and decent fiber of my being not to go ballistic each time I saw him.

But, today, as Charlotte had been talking about me in the courtroom, I'd watched Brady's face. And every single positive word she had said about me had slashed through him like a razor blade.

He was a dick. There was no questioning that. But we did have something in common.

He loved my son.

Our son.

His son.

Travis.

Lucas.

Whatever you wanted to call him.

Brady loved him.

And, right then, just like I was, he was scared out of his fucking mind at the very idea of him going into surgery.

I settled on the edge of the bed and lowered my voice so only Travis could hear me.

"Hey, bud. Can you do me a favor?"

He smiled toothy and wide. "Sure, Dad."

I rested my hand on his forearm and gave him a squeeze. "Do you remember that time that you really wanted to buy some coins on that game on your iPad but you weren't sup-posed to get your allowance for another week?"

"But they were on sale." He laughed.

"Right," I whispered. "They were on sale, so I gave you an advance on your allowance so you could buy them."

"Yeah," he drawled. "That was so awesome."

I chuckled. "So, here's the thing, bud. Brady and Charlotte love you a lot. And I know you don't necessarily love them yet, but I promise you will one day. I was wondering if maybe you could give them an advance on that love before you go in and get that new ticker of yours. You know, just to make them feel better."

"I like Charlotte." He shrugged. "I could love her."

I smiled. "That's good to hear."

"Brady's nice and all, but—"

"It's just an advance, Trav. It would mean a lot to them."

He stared at me, unfocused for several seconds, then smiled. "Okay, then."

God, I loved my son.

My vision began to swim, but I refused the tears their release. This was not a sad day.

It was a day for smiles and laughs.

For hopes and dreams.

For futures and celebration.

But, most of all, it was a day for new beginnings.

"Hey, Brady," Travis croaked.

Brady became unstuck from the corner. "I'm right here, Travis."

"I…just wanted to say…" He flicked his gaze to mine and then back to Brady. "That I love you."

I patted my son's hand, pride soaring inside me.

Charlotte gasped.

Brady's whole body locked up tight. His eyes grew wide almost as quickly as they filled with tears. He coughed and then cleared his throat. "I love you too."

"You got to be nicer to Charlotte," Travis continued, and I tucked my head low and chuckled.

"Oh…uh…yeah, okay," Brady breathed.

"She's pretty awesome when you get to know her. She'd be way cooler if she got a TV for her apartment. But at least she has Wi-Fi."

Charlotte stepped forward and took his hand. "I promise.

As soon as we get a new house, we'll get a TV."

Travis shot her a wide smile. "Okay, then I don't have to give you an advance when I tell you that I love you."

She nodded at least a dozen times. Her face did that scrunchy trying-not-to-cry-and-failing thing she did so often. It usually made me laugh, and this was no different.

Taking her hand in mine, I guided her to stand between my legs.

"I love you too," she whispered through tears.

"Don't cry." He laughed. "Go ahead. You can call me Lucas if it will make you feel better."

Her face softened and somehow turned sad even as she smiled. "I don't want to call you Lucas. If you're Travis, then I love *you*, Travis."

He stared at her, his drunken gaze flashing with a moment of clarity. "Really?"

She wrapped her hand over his and lifted her hands to her mouth to kiss his knuckles. "Of course. I don't want you to be anyone else. I love *you*."

There was no mistaking the honesty in her voice.

My throat burned with unshed emotion.

It was amazing the way children could heal you with such simple words.

If only our words could have healed him.

Ten minutes later, anesthesia finally arrived. With kisses, hugs, and whispered good-lucks, we left our son in the hands of the transplant team. Charlotte stayed with Travis, while Brady and I were escorted to a waiting room where most of our family had already congregated.

Tanner and Rita were there. My mom had stayed home

to keep Hannah, but she had sent Dad with strict instructions to text her every ten minutes. Charlotte's mom and Tom were there, along with some faces I didn't recognize that I assumed were from Brady's family.

And we were all there for one little boy.

Strapped in and ready to wait out the longest four hours of our lives together.

I'd just finished making my way around the room, receiving hugs and words of encouragement—including a brisk handshake from Tom—when Charlotte finally joined us.

She smiled at her mom and nodded to Tom, but she came straight to me.

"Hi," she whispered, folding her arms around my waist and burying her face in my chest.

"It's going to be okay," I promised, smoothing her long, black hair down.

"I don't think I've ever been this nervous in my life," she confessed.

"I know. Me too."

She peered up at me with glistening eyes. "Thank you for that in there."

I played dumb. "For what?"

"I don't know what kind of *advance* you had to promise him, but to hear him say, 'I love you,' I'd gladly pay it a thousandfold."

I tucked a stray hair behind her ear. "I didn't pay him anything. That was the truth."

"Even the part where he chastised Brady for not being nice to me?"

"*Actually*, yes. I had nothing to do with that."

She sighed. "God, I love that kid."

"That makes…" I popped my head up and looked around the room. "A lot of us."

She giggled soft and sad. "I'm really glad the judge allowed you to be here."

"Christ, me too. Hey, that reminds me." I dipped low and kissed her slow and sweet.

Arching her back, she curved her body into mine and wrapped her arms around my neck.

"You were incredible in court today. Seriously, Charlotte, if this whole medical thing doesn't work out for you, you could have a career in law."

"I just paid off my medical school loans. I'm not eager to get back into debt for another advanced degree."

I chuckled. "Well, the option is always there."

She blew out a heavy breath and glanced back at the door to the waiting room. "Has it been four hours yet?"

"I wish. I hate the not knowing."

She traced her fingers down my jaw and over my lips. "And Laughlin scrubbed in to observe. He said he'd be sure to keep us in the loop. There will be a nurse who comes in and updates us regularly."

"Not regularly enough," I mumbled. And, when her face fell, I felt guilty about not being stronger and more positive for her. "Hey, you want to play a game?"

"Not particularly."

"Too bad." Taking her hand, I led her over to two chairs situated away from the rest. "Let's pretend."

Her worried eyes flashed dark. "I thought we said no more pretending."

I kissed her forehead and then murmured, "But this is the good kind of pretending." I turned her sideways in her chair and draped her legs over one of my thighs. "The kids and I did this a lot after… Well, anyway. I'll start. Six minutes."

She quirked an eyebrow. "Six minutes to do what?"

"No. Where are we going to be in six minutes?"

"Uh…right here?"

Rolling my eyes, I huffed in mock frustration. "Okay. I'll start. In six minutes from now, we'll still be sitting here, but the nurse will have come in and told us that everything is going well. Brady will drop to his knees, thank the lord, and then stop being an asshole for the rest of our lives."

She grinned. "Psh… Good luck with that."

"Now, you go. Six hours from now…."

She blinked. "Um…six hours from now, we'll be…" She stopped talking, and tears filled her eyes.

"It's okay," I breathed, rubbing her back. "Nothing is too big to wish for during Six Minutes."

She nodded and swallowed. "Okay…so, six hours from now, we'll be sitting in Travis's recovery room, waiting for him to wake up, while listening to his new heart play a perfect rhythm on the monitors."

"Damn right we will." I winked. "Now, my turn. Six days from now…" I tapped on my chin. "It'll be me and you, dressed all in black. I'm talking ski masks, cargo pants, black Henleys, combat boots—the whole nine."

"So, we're robbing a bank? What is it with you always breaking the law? Do you have a crew you need to get back to in jail?"

I laughed when it should have been impossible. "Nope.

We're sneaking Hannah in to see her brother."

"Ah…we should probably get a giant duffel bag."

"See? You know what I'm talking about!"

"Though, on second thought, it would probably be easier if I walked her in through the door. Six days from now, he'll be out of ICU and in the transplant unit. I know some people who can get us in as long as she's not sick and he's healing up properly."

"Oh. Well." I scoffed. "Now, you're just showing off."

Her shoulder shook with laughter and she beamed up at me. "I love you so much."

"I know." I winked. "Now, six weeks. You're up."

"Humm…six weeks. Well, we'll be home from the hospital."

"Whose home?" I clarified.

"Uh…my new one."

I made the sound of an annoying buzzer. "Wrong answer."

She twisted her lips. "Okay… Your house?"

I did the buzzer thing again. "Still wrong!"

"Whose house, then?"

I leaned in close and brushed her lips with mine. "*Our* house."

"What? No." She jerked away, but I caught the back of her neck to prevent her from going far.

"You need a bigger place," I whispered. "I happen to *have* a bigger place."

She gripped my wrist, her fingers biting into it as she held it tight. "We can't just move in together."

"Why not?" I asked. "It solves all of our problems."

"Only by creating more problems. What if we don't work

out? The kids would be devastated."

"So we'll work out."

Her panicked gaze searched mine. "It's not that easy."

"It *is* that easy. It's a commitment. To each other. To the kids. To being a family. Look, I know it's going to be hard *sometimes* and we'll go through our ups and downs like any other couple, but come on, Charlotte. I'm thinking, after all of this, there isn't much we couldn't conquer together."

She began gnawing on her bottom lip. "I don't know."

"Yeah, you do. Think about it. Travis gets to go back to the house and bedroom he calls home. You yourself said today that this stress is not good for him. Imagine what another move could do while he's trying to recover? And, this way, he gets to keep both of us close. On the nights when you're working at the hospital, he'll have me there. And, on the nights when I'm at the restaurant, you'll be there. And, on nights when we're both there, we'll be together like a family."

She cut her eyes over my shoulder. "You're talking a lot about the kids, but what about us, Porter?"

"Us?" I laughed. "Sweetheart, *we* are the easiest part of this. I love you. You love me. I get to fall asleep every night with you in my arms. I get to make love to you in the darkness. And hold you in the light. I don't have to crawl out of your bed to rush home. We don't have to make time for each other when our schedules get too busy. We can finally be together."

She shook her head, short and jerky. "It's too soon."

"That's what the six weeks are for, crazy," I teased.

She half laughed, half cried. "You're the crazy one."

"I'll gladly accept that title as long as you're planning to move in with me."

She peeked up at me with timid eyes. "I don't—"

The whole room jumped when the door suddenly swung open.

Travis's surgeon was standing on the other side, his face pale and filled with sorrow.

Greg Laughlin stepped in behind him, his face contorted in agony, his eyes aimed on Charlotte.

They weren't supposed to be there.

They were supposed to be in the middle of surgery.

On my son.

They were supposed to be giving him a new heart.

Giving him a second chance at life.

They were *not* supposed to be standing there with apology in their eyes.

"Charlotte," Greg called before swallowing hard.

"No," she whispered.

He swept his gaze through the room, stalling on Tanner and Rita for a beat, but the pain in his eyes was stronger than ever when it landed on Charlotte.

"Maybe we should talk in the hall," he whispered.

On shaking legs, Charlotte rose to her feet, her eyes feral. "You are not here right now."

"I'm sorry," he whispered.

"You are not here right now!" she repeated, her tears finally breaching the surface.

Every hair on my body stood on end, and nausea rolled in my stomach.

"No!" she screamed. That single word was so tortured that it was as though it had been torn from her soul.

And, as it ricocheted around the room, it tore through mine.

I couldn't breathe. I couldn't think. I couldn't focus.

My legs wouldn't work, and my arms were slack at my sides.

It felt as though every part of my body were simultaneously being ripped off while I was being stabbed with a million hot irons.

Greg moved fast and was on Charlotte in a second. His arms wrapped around her, keeping her on her feet, while his mouth moved at her ear.

The room erupted in a flurry of cries and questions.

But I couldn't hear anything over the thunder of my own pulse.

I sat there, unable to move, desperately trying to figure how it was possible for the darkness to get even darker.

TWENTY

Charlotte

T HE ROOM WAS PITCH BLACK.

The darkest night even before the sun had sunk on the horizon.

We'd been sitting like that for a while. I was in his lap, my legs draped over the arm of the chair, and his arms around my back.

Our hearts beat in unison.

Our breaths mingled in the inches between us.

The tears had dried hours ago.

But the fear and the uncertainty were more potent than ever.

"What do we do now?" he whispered.

"We just keep holding on to each other," I choked out. Unable to see, I felt his head fall back as he stared up at the ceiling.

"How?"

My breathing shuddered. Porter had always been so strong for me. I had to be there for him now. I owed him that much.

"Did I ever tell you about my first sunrise after he went missing?"

He shook his head, sad and slow.

I curled closer into him as if I could somehow get inside and ease the staggering aches in both of our hearts.

"The day Lucas was taken, I overheard Brady tell my mom that only two percent of children who had been kidnapped come home after the first twenty-four hours. I didn't think much of it at the time because my son was coming back to me. You know? But, as time wore on...I wasn't so sure anymore. I began to obsess about that clock. After I got home from the police station that night, my mom helped me change out of my clothes. I'd been too consumed mentally, physically, and emotionally with the second hand on the clock to perform even the most basic of tasks. Each silent click of that tiny, plastic arm was deafening." My voice hitched as the memory of that day slayed me. "Time was running out. I was only hours from becoming the part of the ninety-eight percent who never saw their child alive again."

"Charlotte," he whispered. "Don't go back there."

"I have to," I breathed, touching my lips to his.

He sighed and silently waited for me to continue.

"I was one sunrise and two percentage points away from a lifetime of the unfathomable—being forced to carry on without him. It was all so surreal. I couldn't sleep that night. And, with another tick from the clock, I feared I'd never be able to sleep again. Not without him. So I threw on a pair of shoes and climbed out the window like I was sixteen again.

"I can still remember the chill in the air assaulting me, though it was still infinitely warmer than the frozen tundra icing over my heart. Where I was going, I wasn't sure, but I couldn't sit there doing nothing anymore. He was out there somewhere without me. My feet started moving on their own accord toward the park. The same path, step for step, that I'd taken earlier that morning with my son before the world had turned upside down. My hands ached for the stroller handle, and my ears yearned to hear the cries I'd so desperately been trying to silence with that morning walk. In that minute, I'd have given anything to have those cries back." My body tensed, the regret and longing in the memory becoming tangible all over again.

Porter nuzzled my jaw with his breath whispering over me like the softest feather. "I'm right here, Charlotte. I've got you."

I inhaled so deeply that my lungs ached, and then I continued. "As my legs carried me closer to the place I'd last seen him, I allowed my mind to conjure up memories of that trip. It was crazy… When I had left my house that morning, I was frustrated, sleep-deprived, and impatient, but in hindsight, I'd never been happier in my life." My voice cracked.

But Porter silently held me and allowed me the time to collect myself.

"I talked to him," I confessed. Closing my eyes, I allowed my mind to transport me back in time. "Little things, like, 'Shh… It's okay, baby. Mamma's right here.' I whispered them into the wind as if he could hear me. But, with a silent scream from yet another second passing me by, hope slipped further and further out of my reach. That night, I sat on the bench for hours, pretending the sun was still high in the sky, children running and laughing all around us, Lucas crying in his stroller." I paused as my chin began to quiver and the traitorous tears once again hit my eyes. "But, most of all, I pretended I'd never let him out of my sight."

"Sweetheart," Porter soothed, gliding a hand up and down my back.

"I stayed there all night. My eyes aimed at the horizon. And, regardless of how hard I tried, I couldn't stop the sun from rising that morning. It was the darkest sunrise of my entire life. For ten years, I lived and breathed that darkness every day until I found you."

"Jesus, Charlotte." He palmed each side of my face and kissed me. His lips were full of love and tasted of hope.

"It's always darkest before dawn, Porter. We just have to wait a little while longer. The sun always rises, baby."

"Dad?" Travis croaked, and we both exploded out of the chair.

"Yeah...I'm here, buddy. Charlotte too," Porter said, smoothing our son's dark hair down.

I flipped the nightlight by the sink on so we could see him.

He'd been asleep for hours. When they had returned him to his room from the OR, he had been awake but still groggy and out of it from the anesthesia. We didn't even have a chance to talk to him before he fell back asleep.

"Is it over? Did I get a new heart?"

Porter took both of our hands in his. "No, buddy. There was something wrong with the donor heart. They didn't even start the surgery."

"Oh," he groaned. "That kinda sucks."

I laughed, a single tear escaping the corner of my eye.

Kinda sucks weren't the words I'd wanted to use when I had seen his surgeon in that doorway.

It had been too soon.

I had known right then and there that there wasn't going to be a transplant that day. Suddenly, I feared there wouldn't ever be one. And, after the drug of hope had swirled so high inside me, the crash back down hit me with a devastating force.

We were right back to the agony of waiting and praying all over again.

It had taken me over thirty minutes of sobbing in Porter's arms to realize that it wasn't over.

There was only one choice.

And, through it all, we would be together.

As long as we held on to that, we couldn't possibly lose.

"Yeah. It definitely sucks," I said softly.

Porter gave my hand a reassuring squeeze. "Hey, what do you say we FaceTime Nana and Hannah? They made me promise to call as soon as you woke up."

"Okay," he mumbled, shifting in the bed. "Since I didn't have the surgery, does that mean I can eat? I'm starving."

"Yeah." I grinned. "I'll make sure the nurse gives you the good red Jell-O."

"Nah, make it green. Hannah loves that stuff."

Smiling, I walked out of that room feeling lighter than I had felt in years.

And it wasn't because everything was finally perfect.

Travis was still in desperate need of a heart.

Brady was still being an ass.

Porter was surely going to push the issue of us moving in together.

But, for me, another day brought another sunrise.

And, for the first time in nearly a decade, I was excited for life on the other side of that horizon.

TWENTY-ONE

Porter

One week later...

"HEY," I SAID, STEPPING OUT IN THE WALKWAY.

Brady froze, one hand on his phone, the other leisurely tucked into the pocket of his khaki slacks. "Hey," he replied, suspiciously flashing his eyes around the area.

I'd been standing outside the hospital entrance for the last half hour, waiting for just that moment. Brady usually arrived at least twenty minutes early to see his son. I'd been trying to catch him alone for the last three days, but I'd missed him every time. Today, it was now or never.

"Can we talk for a minute?" I asked.

His body tightened as he leveled me with a glare. "I'm not sure we have anything to talk about. Save whatever you have to say for the judge."

I stopped in front of him and tilted my head to the side.

"See, that's the thing. The judge and I don't have any issues at the moment. Everything I have to say is for *you*."

"Okay, let me rephrase. I'm not interested in anything you have to say. I'm just trying to see my son. So, if you'll excuse me—"

I shifted my weight between my feet and crossed my arms over my chest. "I'm withdrawing my petition for partial custody."

His eyebrows shot up, and his chin jerked to the side. "I'm sorry. Come again?"

Yeah. That was basically my family's reaction when I'd told them earlier that morning. They'd all been certain I was losing my mind. Deep down, I knew I was doing the right thing.

"Travis was four when I first met him," I announced. "I was on this new health kick and decided I was going to eat all organic and local produce." I chuckled.

Brady glared at me impatiently.

"I'll never forget. I was picking out tomatoes when I caught him staring at me. He had these big, brown eyes, but his face was completely blank." I smiled and cut my gaze down to the ground. "Now, knowing Charlotte, it makes a lot more sense."

"Can you get to the point?" he grumbled.

I took another step toward him. "The point is I had to build a relationship with him too. What Travis and I have was not a natural thing in the beginning. I had to work for it. Day in and day out, I put in the time to grow something with him. Yeah, he was younger then, but that doesn't mean I didn't have to earn his trust. I started from scratch, Brady. Just like you. So I know it's possible. But you've lost your fucking mind if you

221

don't think he feels the tension between us."

His jaw ticked as he stared at me with an interesting mixture of frustration and rapt interest. "The tension between us wouldn't exist if you weren't always in the room…even when you're not."

"Yeah, Charlotte mentioned that he's been throwing my name around with you a lot. And I'm going to talk to him about that. But, Brady, you have to recognize that's his defense mechanism. He knows you and I don't get along and he feels like he has to pick sides."

"And that's what pisses me off the most. I have to fucking compete with you for even the smallest morsel of his affection." He pointed at the hospital entrance behind me. "That is my son."

I threw my hands out to my sides and slapped them against my thighs as they fell. "Then don't make it a competition."

He scoffed. "Right. 'Cause it's just that easy."

"Yes," I implored. "It is that easy."

"Bullshit."

"Charlotte's moving in with me," I announced.

His eyes grew wide and murderous. "What?"

"She's going to tell you today. And I swear to God, Brady. You give her a single syllable of shit about it, I have no problem going back to jail."

His eyes narrowed. "So, you two are just going to set up shop, play house, and act like one big, happy fucking family?"

"No. We aren't going to *act* like anything. We're going to *be* one big, happy family. And this is me asking you to be a part of that family with us."

"Oh, you got a spare bedroom for me and Steph?" he

asked, his voice thick with sarcasm.

I glowered. "Don't be a dick right now. I'm extending an olive branch here."

"Well, keep your fucking olive branch. You and Charlotte can do whatever the fuck you want, because when this shit is done, my son is coming home with me."

I caught his arm when he tried to walk away. "Why won't you let her be happy?"

"This has nothing to do with Charlotte," he snapped, yanking his arm from my grasp.

"It has *everything* to do with her. You've spent ten years blaming her for Catherine kidnapping Lucas. She's paid the price. But I swear to you, Brady, you push this custody issue, you're going to be the one to pay the price next."

He tipped his chin up and did his best to get in my face. "Don't fucking threaten me."

"I'm not threatening you. I'm stating facts." I lifted a single finger in the air. "One, the judge is never going to award you full custody. Charlotte's a damn good mother. And you know it." I flipped another digit up. "And two, you are going to ruin any possible relationship you have with Travis if you try to push this."

"You move in with Charlotte and I'm already ruined!" he yelled. "Fuck! You think he's going to be real eager to come to my house when he has his perfect little family at home?"

"Brady, I'm going to say this one more time. I'm *not* your competition. You got a wife. You got another son. Make him a happy little family at your house too. People do blended families all the time."

"But I'm the stepdad in this equation. He looks at me and

Stephanie like we're strangers."

"Because you *are* strangers to him. *For now.* But you have all the tools to make that change. Look, I'm willing to take the first step to make this work for everyone involved. If Charlotte and I are together, there is no reason for us to have to split custody three ways. I'll bow out in court. But *only* in court. We have to find a way to make this work because I'm going to be a part of your son's life from now until the day I die. I'm going to marry Charlotte, Brady. Maybe not today, and if she has any say in it, maybe not even six months from now. But I'm going to do it. And, right now, I'm giving you the opportunity to be a part of that family too."

He stared at me, his lips tight and thin, his hands fisted on his hips. "What are you asking me to do right now?"

I breathed in deep and held his stare. "Drop your petition for full custody. Let's show Travis that we're on the same damn team. You, Stephanie, me, Charlotte, and Travis sit down and figure out an arrangement that works for all of us." I hooked my thumb at the entrance. "We still have a long road to go in this place. But I think it would do a lot for his mental health to at least know what was going to happen when he does get to come home."

"The same team?" he scoffed.

"Yeah, Brady. The *same* team. *His* team. You don't have to like me. But let our son see that we aren't enemies. He trusts me. Make it so he doesn't feel like he's caught in the middle of us. Only then will you have any hopes of building the relationship you want with him. Stop making this about you and me. Or you and Charlotte. We're all just here for Travis."

He swallowed hard and raked a hand through the top of

his hair. "I don't know how to do this. No matter what I do, you're always going to be his dad."

"Yeah. But so are you. We have a lot more in common than you think, Brady. There's room for both of us in his life." I grinned. "I'll even let you be the cool dad who takes him fun places and allows him to stay up until midnight eating chocolate and drinking Mountain Dew." I lifted a finger in the air, walked back to the corner where I'd been waiting, and retrieved my bag. "Here."

He dipped his gaze to the bag but didn't take it. "What's that?"

"That, my friend, is a special-edition Minecraft Diamond Ore nightlight. Six months ago, they were forty-nine ninety-nine online. Today, they are two hundred and fifty dollars on eBay."

"Jesus," Brady mumbled.

"My thoughts exactly. But he's been asking for it since the day it came out. And, by the time I broke down and agreed to buy it, you couldn't find the damn things anywhere." I shook the bag at him. "Take it."

He glanced down and shook his head. "I don't want to buy his affections."

"You're not. You're going to use this to buy mine."

His head snapped up. "What?"

"Travis isn't stupid. We go up there and pretend everything is hunky-dory, he's not going to believe it. If you take this up there, he's going to know it's a gift and he's going to want it real bad, but since it's coming from you, he's going to be hesitant. But I won't be. I'll go on and on about how much it cost and how they are impossible to find and how cool it is when it lights up for all of ten minutes, whatever. You're going to go on and on about how you found it on eBay and got into a bidding war with Dan TDM over it." I paused to repeat myself slowly. "Dan T-D-M. He's some YouTube personality. Write it down. That's the part that will win you some cool points."

He blinked and then slipped a hand into his pocket before pulling a pen out.

"I'm going to thank you. You and I are going to shake hands. And then Travis and I are going to sit on the bed and play with it."

His head shot back again. "Shouldn't it be Travis and I sitting on the bed playing with it?"

"No. Because, while I'm sitting there with him, he's going to be watching *you*. Everything that comes out of his mouth over the next hour will be a test. He's going to push your buttons—hard and repeatedly. He's going to call me dad more than you can count. He's going to tell all of his favorite stories about growing up. If Charlotte steps out, he might even bring Catherine into it. All just waiting for you to show any sign of anger or frustration." I leaned in close and lowered my voice. "Show him nothing and I guarantee you the payoff will be huge."

Our eyes locked in a standoff. I could almost see the gears turning in his head. I had to give him credit. He desperately wanted that relationship with our son. He just couldn't figure out how to put all the bullshit aside long enough to make it happen.

He sighed but finally took the bag. "I don't know that I can drop the issue of custody."

"That's fine. Just think about it. Play this my way today

and I'll prove to you how good it could be if he felt safe to love all of us."

He cut his gaze over my shoulder and scratched the back of his head. "I'm not the fucking bad guy here. I want what's best for my son."

"We all do. And I can assure you, if we all work together, that best will be better."

Brady stared at me for several seconds before nodding. "Let's give this toy business a shot. I'm willing to do anything at this point."

I smiled.

He glared.

But, in the end, we shared an elevator up to the fourth floor.

TWENTY-TWO

Charlotte

Two weeks later...

"WHAT DID YOU DO?" I ACCUSED INTO PORTER'S MOUTH as I slipped the bra straps down my arms.

"Nothing," he mumbled, trailing openmouthed kisses up and down my neck.

My bra hadn't even hit the floor before he took my nipples between his fingers, plucking and rolling.

Gripping his shoulders for balance, I threw my head back and opened my legs.

His hand slipped down and popped the button on my jeans open. Then he scooped my panties out of the way before his fingers dipped inside.

"Yesss," I hissed, teetering on the edge of my desk.

It was after hours and we were there to clean my office out, but the moment the door shut and we had the barest hint of privacy, that notion had quickly dissolved.

After much debate, Greg and I had decided that it would be best to take on another doctor at North Point Pulmonology. Travis was still in the hospital, waiting for a heart, and while I definitely needed more time off to take care of him, the fact of the matter was that I was never going back to work.

At least, not in the same way I'd been working over the last few years.

I had a family now. People who needed and depended on me. People who weren't my patients. I would never give medicine up. I loved it and it was the only thing that had kept me sane for all those years when Lucas had been missing. But it was time for a change.

My job was never going to be nine to five. People didn't look at the clock before they got sick. But there was such a thing as balancing my professional life and my home life. I'd decided to cut back on my patient load, and if I wanted to cut back on my on-call hours too, we'd need more help.

Dr. Franklin was an amazing addition to our team, but until we could find a new building for our growing practice, she needed an office. And, because I was extending my leave of absence, I'd offered her mine.

Though, given the clench I was currently in with Porter, I was probably going to need to sanitize the desk for her before I left. But I couldn't bring myself to care. After weeks of passing like two ships in the night, I wasn't about to delay that moment in search of a bed.

"Fuck, you're ready for me," he breathed, gliding his fingers inside me.

I moaned and pressed my lips to his mouth. "So, let me

get this straight," I whispered, sliding my hand down to his zipper and then over his hard length. "Brady just happened to change his motion from full custody to joint custody one day before we're slated to go to court?"

"Dear God, are you seriously talking about Brady right now?" he rumbled, stilling his hand.

I moved my assault to his neck, kissing my way up before nipping at his ear. "Admit you had something to do with this."

"I had something to do with this," he replied immediately. Then he removed his fingers and snatched my pants down my legs.

"I knew it. Have you been talking to Travis about him too? He's been so much more open to Brady recently."

Porter groaned. "Woman, I have not been inside you in five days. For the love of all that's holy, stop talking about Brady and the kids."

I giggled, but it morphed into a moan as he freed himself from his jeans and guided himself into my opening.

Reclining across the desk, I arched my back and circled my hips as he planted himself deep. And then there were no more words as our bodies took over and relished in the connection we both so desperately needed.

Over the last few weeks, we'd had our ups and downs. Travis was sick of living at the hospital, but his body was too weak to go home. His frustration was palpable, and he'd started taking it out on all of us. We'd been doing our best to keep him comfortable, but come on…hospitals suck.

Hannah was also having a hard time adapting to the disruption in her family. She missed Porter and Travis more than her young mind could express, and it wasn't long before she, too, started acting out. I felt so bad for Porter. He had two children who desperately needed him, but there was only one of him. And, regardless of how hard he tried, he couldn't be everywhere. I pitched in as much as I could, but there was no substitute for their dad.

And the kids weren't alone in their struggles to adapt. Porter and I had both taken turns falling into the lows of fear and worry. But, through it all, we'd leaned on each other.

When I broke, Porter was there to pick up the pieces.

And, when Porter lost sight of the light, I was there to hold him in the darkness.

No questions.

No judgments.

No faking it.

No apologies.

Our lives were far from perfect, but the fact that we were living and not standing still as the world turned beneath our feet made it perfect to us.

Porter came on the muffled groan of my name, and moments later, I followed him down in a crash of ecstasy.

"Jesus," he breathed, peppering kisses over my face and neck.

Smiling, I raked my nails up and down his back. His skin pebbled and he squirmed as I teased at his sides.

"Ya know…I only promised her an office. I didn't say anything about there being a desk."

"Excellent call. We can throw this baby in the Tahoe and put it with the couch from my office. I can see it now. The bonus room could become a shrine for all the places we've had sex."

"That wouldn't be awkward at all," I teased.

"I have it on good authority that you like awkward," he mumbled, begrudgingly pulling out of me as he started to soften.

After a long discussion, I'd finally given in and agreed to move in with Porter. It really did make sense. I was still terrified, but it had been next to impossible to tell him no when I could feel his excitement vibrating in the air between us. Since I had until the end of the month to be out, we'd decided to slowly move my stuff into Porter's house. But, a few days later, I'd learned that the word *slow* had a vastly different meaning to him. One afternoon, after I'd come home from the hospital to take a shower, I'd boxed a few things up to start the merger of our lives. I'd given Porter my keys and asked him to pick them up on his way home. The next day, I'd walked through my front door to find a herd of professional movers and a nearly empty apartment.

We'd fought—okay, fine. *I'd* fought. Porter had just smiled. A lot.

We'd been officially living together for over a week and not once had we slept under the same roof. One of us was always up at the hospital—usually me so Porter could stay at home with Hannah.

It was exhausting, but none of that mattered. Not as long as we had each other.

The office was empty as I walked back from the bathroom after having cleaned up. It was funny—I'd spent so much of my time in that building, years of my life spent growing that place into the thriving pulmonology practice it had become, but I wasn't going to miss it.

Sure, I'd be back, but when I walked through those doors again, I'd be doing it as a different person.

The broken, lost-in-the-darkness version of Charlotte Mills was gone. And I couldn't have been happier about the future without her.

Pushing my office door open, I found Porter standing at my desk, staring at his phone.

He didn't look up as he said, "Six minutes. You go first."

I smiled at the ridiculous game I knew he'd made up that day at the hospital to distract me. But such was Porter. He did a lot of things just to make me smile when it should have been impossible.

Swaying my hips, I sauntered over to him. "Six minutes from now, we'll be in the car, on the way back to *our* house to drop this stuff off." I ducked under his arm and pressed my front against his side while circling my arms around his waist.

He finally looked up from his phone and it felt as though the air had become electrified. His face was tight, and his jaw was clenched. But his eyes—God, I will never forget his eyes—were filled with light.

"Porter?" I whispered.

"Six hours from now, we'll be sitting in the recovery room with Travis. Listening to the sound of his new heart beating on a monitor." His voice broke and his shoulders shook, but it was a loud and joyous laugh that sprang from his throat.

Nerves and excitement ignited inside me as the hairs on the back of my neck stood on end. "What?" I breathed.

He smiled down at me. "They're prepping him for surgery now. We need to get up to the hospital."

My face crumbled, but through it all, a smile grew on my

lips. "Seriously?" I asked in disbelief that it was finally happening, and hopefully for real this time.

Porter's eyes filled with more love than I had known existed in the world only a few months earlier. And then he dipped low, and with one touch of his lips, he transferred it all to me.

"Seriously, sweetheart."

• ▸•⬦•◂ •

We were alone in the darkness.

The place where it had all started.

And the place where we were desperately hoping it would end.

I was in his lap, our breaths mingling as silence filled the air.

There were no confessions to make.

It had been four hours since the nurse had come in to tell us that they had started the surgery.

And two hours since she had come back to inform us that his heart had been removed.

With the exception of the day when I'd realized he'd gone missing, I'd never been more terrified in my life. Whether his body accepted the new heart or not, there was no turning back.

But that was exactly the thing with our lives—none of us wanted to go back. Our hopes and dreams were all about the future laid out in front of us.

Images of Travis graduating high school and attending his first prom illuminated the backs of my eyelids.

Visions of Porter holding my hand as he grew older, his hair turning gray but his infectious smile never fading.

Hannah blossoming into a young woman who loved sleepovers, makeup, and giggling about boys until three a.m.

And me experiencing it all right along with them, embracing every moment of the beauty I never thought I'd have.

Porter nuzzled my jaw and I closed my eyes, reveling in the warmth as it cascaded over me, driving out the chill of reality.

No questions.

No judgments.

No faking it.

No apologies.

We both jumped as the door cracked open.

The darkness parted to make way for the light.

Sticks and stones will break my bones, but words will never harm me.

Lies.

Syllables and letters may not be tangible, but they can still destroy your entire life faster than a bullet from a gun.

However, they can also heal your wounds, tethering parts of your heart back together when all hope seemed lost.

Words weren't always the weapon.

They were sometimes the sweetest remedy.

Nine words. That was all it took to bathe my entire world in the brightest light imaginable.

"He did great. Everything's going to be just fine."

EPILOGUE

Charlotte

"**T**HIS ISN'T FAIR!" TRAVIS COMPLAINED FOR approximately the four hundredth time since the party had started.

Two number one candles were glowing from the top of his chocolate cake, illuminating his face as the purples and pinks of the sunset behind him faded into darkness.

Various shades of blue, green, and brown streamers—Minecraft colors—decorated the deck at our new house. We'd only been there for a few months, but it was more of a home than I'd had in over a decade. That had little to do with the five-bedroom, three-bath house Porter and I had picked out together and everything to do with the three people who shared it with me.

While Porter had convinced me to move in with him, I'd still had a few reservations. And, only weeks after I'd officially changed my address, I'd figured out what they were. Catherine might not have been a part of his house, but as I'd stood on our front porch watching Hannah collect fireflies in a pickle jar, the small one-story house Porter had shared with his ex-wife had taunted me from the end of the cul-de-sac.

She didn't get to be a part of that beauty. Not even in memories. At least, not mine.

Porter, being the amazingly understanding man he always had been, didn't bat an eye when I'd confessed in the darkness my desire to move. The very next afternoon, I'd sat in his lap at the kitchen table and scanned the listings our real estate agent had emailed over.

We bought the first house we looked at. It was everything we had never known we wanted. It was further out than we had planned to move—at least thirty minutes from each of our offices. But it was nowhere near Porter's bridge or Lucas's park. Just the way we liked it. Though what really sold me on the property was the clear view of the horizon off the expansive back deck.

Every morning, the rising sun would flood the living room in light. And it was just far enough outside the city that, each night, after the sun had disappeared, the stars danced in the sky, proving that there was always light to be found—even in the darkness.

Travis peered at his father from over the top of his cake. "I already had an eleventh birthday. I'm twelve!"

"I'm with you, bud." Porter flicked his gaze to mine, and his bright, white smile nearly blinded me. "It's Charlotte here who insists you're only eleven." He rested his hand on top of mine, but instead of intertwining our fingers, he used his thumb to play with the large, round diamond on my engagement ring.

Porter had proposed in the most Porter way possible.

Sweet, charming, romantic, and completely ridiculous.

Two weeks after we'd moved into the new house, I'd run to the grocery store to pick up something for dinner. When I'd arrived home, I'd opened the front door and then jumped back at least three feet, dropping all of my bags to the floor. Waiting for me on the other side of the door had been a life-size cardboard cutout of Porter wearing a…

Wait for it…

Pink speedo. His hands were on his hips and he was staring straight ahead with a sexy smoldering gaze. Written across his chest in what appeared to be white sunscreen was: *Ian who?* Once my heart had slowed, I laughed wildly and retrieved the cocktail napkin taped to his shoulder. On it was a hand-drawn map of our house, complete with arrows guiding me toward the kitchen. Suspiciously, I called for Porter and the kids, but when they didn't answer, I followed the map to our pantry, where I found yet another cardboard cutout. This time, Porter was wearing jeans and a black T-shirt that read: *Charlotte's Boyfriend. (Whether she likes it or not.)* In his hand was a burger with a little toothpick flag on the top that read: *Wagyu Terrier.*

My mouth had split into an epic grin, but realization that this was more than just one of Porter's usual silly stunts dawned on me, causing my stomach to flutter. I plucked yet another cocktail napkin map off his shoulder and followed the directions down the hall to our bedroom. With caution, I pushed the door open and found yet another cardboard cutout. This one wasn't Porter. Or maybe it was—but only his dark silhouette. Across the chest, it read: *Porter in the Darkness.*

Tears welled in my eyes and nerves ignited in my veins, but I once again took the cocktail napkin off his shoulder. The map pointed to our closet.

With a racing pulse, I slowly opened the door and then burst into loud laughter. There were three cardboard cutouts. One of me and Porter taken God knew where, but he was staring straight ahead, his arm draped over my shoulders, his wide signature smile splitting his lips. The cardboard version of me was laughing beside him. And not the attractive kind. My mouth was open, my eyes were squeezed closed, and I had my arm bent so I could hold his hand where it was dangling over my chest. On his left was a cutout of Hannah. She was wearing her favorite pink floral dress paired with horrible red-and-white leggings. Her dark hair had been braided into pigtails, and she, too, was in the middle of what I was positive was a loud belly laugh. A cutout of Travis was on my right. He was wearing his typical uniform: neon basketball shorts and a plain colored T-shirt. His chin was tipped up in the air, his arms crossed over his chest, and he was smirking like a little man.

My gaze drifted back to Porter, where I noticed the words written across the front of his shirt: *Porter in the light.*

My chest warmed and my heart swelled as it filled with love. I looked ridiculous in that silly cardboard cutout, but that was Charlotte in the light too.

After taking the cocktail napkin map, I followed it down the hall to the sliding glass back door. There, on the deck, was another version of paper-Porter. But this one stole my breath. He was gorgeous in a black tux that fit him like a glove. His jacket was open, and his right hand was shoved inside his pocket. He was smiling the way he always did, but this was the heated grin Porter reserved for me when we were alone.

My lungs seized, and that warmth in my chest spread through the rest of my body like a wildfire.

His left hand was resting over his heart, and on his ring finger was a thick, gold band.

There was one of those "Hello My Name is" tags stuck on the lapel of his jacket and it read: *Porter in the Future.*

Tears escaped my eyes as I slapped a hand over my mouth.

Porter had made no secret of how much he wanted us to become a family. He'd even bought a rustic wooden picture frame, which he'd hung in the entryway, engraved with the words: *The Reese family: Porter, Charlotte, Travis, and Hannah.*

After I'd lived frozen in time for almost ten years, change scared the absolute shit out of me. But I had to admit that the idea of marrying Porter did some seriously good things to my heart.

However, for as many times as he'd talked about us getting married, he'd never actually proposed.

Until that moment.

I peeled the cocktail napkin map off cardboard-Porter's shoulder only to find it blank. Drying my tears on my shoulder, I flipped it over. Written in thick, black ink were the words: *Turn around.*

With my heart in my throat, I spun faster than I knew possible.

And then the tears came full force.

Over the years, I'd cried a lot.

But these were different.

They were good tears. Happy tears. Yes-I'll-marry-you tears.

In the same tux, the real Porter was down on one knee. Ring box open. A diamond sparkling in the sunlight. The biggest, most beautiful smile I'd seen him wear splitting his mouth. And a "Hello My Name is…" tag on his jacket read: *Porter in the present.*

He didn't say anything.

We just stood there staring at each other.

Finally, when the silence became too much, I choked out through tears, "Are you going to ask me or what?"

His smile stretched. "I think I might have been a little premature when I asked for just a little company in the darkness."

I laughed, and it turned into more tears. "Ya think?"

He rose and walked toward me, removing the ring from the box. He stopped in front of me and took my hand in his. "Charlotte Mills, I'd like to spend a lifetime with you. In the darkness. In the light. And everywhere in between. Forever." He leaned forward and whispered in my ear, "Marry me."

It wasn't a question, and he didn't wait for my answer before sliding the ring on my finger.

I said yes all the same.

And, two weeks later, we were married in a small, family-only ceremony at Tanner's pond. I'd had a lot of incredible days that year, but vowing my life to Porter was certainly near the top.

I smiled at our son, doing my best to tamp the emotion down. "I'm sorry, Trav. Just pretend you found a time machine."

Brady barked a laugh from the corner, where he stood

behind his wife, his arms draped around her midsection and his hands resting on top of her swelling stomach. They had found out only a week earlier that it was another boy. Judging by the way Stephanie stared at Hannah, I knew she'd been hoping for a girl. I also knew she'd love that baby no matter what.

Things with Brady were…well, different.

Legally, we shared custody of our son—fifty-fifty. But, after Travis's transplant, it had been virtually impossible for him to travel back and forth between our houses. Brady hated it at first, but we all agreed Travis's health was our number-one priority. I thought Brady was going to swallow his tongue when Porter told the entire Boyd family that our door was *always* open for them. As much as Brady hated the idea, we didn't have any other options. It was awkward at first, but I should have known that my man excelled at awkward.

The first time Brady and his family came over after Travis had come home, Porter had a big meal delivered from The Porterhouse. The visit was strained, with a lot of uncomfortable conversations and forced smiles, but it was more than I'd ever hoped for with Brady. While his attitude had changed over the last few months, Brady and I were never going to be best friends. From iPad time to nightly desserts, we disagreed on basically everything about raising Travis. But, after the hell we'd lived through and the future laid out in front of us, I'd have been willing to fight with him for the rest of my life about that inconsequential crap.

Travis and Brady's relationship had grown leaps and bounds since the transplant. Porter would always be his dad, but in a way Brady had come to terms with that. He just wanted to be a part of his son's life. As soon as Travis was healthy enough to get out of the house, Porter had told me that he was going to talk to him about giving Brady a real chance. I had no idea what had been said during that discussion, but the following Saturday, Travis invited Brady to go fishing with him. Building a bond between the two of them was going to be a long process, but progress was progress.

Flashing our son a teasing grin, Brady said, "You should count your blessings, big man. I suggested we make you start back at one."

Desperate for some kind of backup, Travis turned to Tom. "Isn't there some kind of law…"

"Hey, hey, hey! Kid, don't drag me into the middle of this!" Tom joked. "Charlotte almost kicked me out the last time I sided with you."

"That's because everyone knows mustard is the superior condiment!" I exclaimed, making nearly everyone in the room gag.

Tanner sauntered onto the deck, a beer in his hand, the faintest tint of red lipstick smeared on his lips. "Let's not get carried away, Charlotte."

I glanced over just in time to see Rita walk out behind him, dabbing at her lips.

"Sloth, don't start with me," I clipped.

The room laughed, and I even saw Travis's frown momentarily curl into a secret smile.

Surprisingly enough, despite the early dramas, our families had merged together seamlessly. Lynn and my mom had become fast friends, joining forces in operation Spoil Our Grandchildren Rotten. And, yes, that was *grandchildren*. My mom had not hesitated in taking Hannah on as her own. I kind of loved her for that. Tom was a little slower on the up-take. It took a few months, but he eventually stopped scowling at Porter, and more recently, I'd even caught them laughing and sharing a beer on the porch. It seemed no one could resist Porter Reese's charm.

I knew I couldn't.

"I seriously have to be eleven for another year?" Travis continued his argument.

"Yes!" we all answered in unison.

The truth was I didn't care what age he was. Just as long as he was there.

It was March seventh and I was celebrating with my family.

That was a miracle in and of itself.

"Blow out the candles, bud," Porter urged.

Travis twisted his lips. "Can I still get that twelve-plus game on my iPad?"

I rolled my eyes. Porter shook his head.

But it was Brady who yelled, "Of course!"

Travis's face lit, and then the candles went dark.

But, for one single second, time stopped and the sun hung in the sky.

I sucked in a sharp breath and reflected on those ten tor-turous years spent in the darkness. Each day leading me closer and closer to the most blinding of lights.

And then time started all over again.

On my son's eleventh birthday, with my husband's hand folded over mine, Travis laughing behind his cake, and a gor-geous little girl who would forever be mine sitting on my lap, I witnessed the brightest sunset of my entire life.

THE END

The Darkest Sunrise Duet

ACKNOWLEDGMENTS

First off, I need to say a HUGE thank you to my Beta Team. They are literally the foundation of every novel I write. They laugh with me, yell at me when I make them cry, and best of all, they are real with me when something sucks.

To: Amie Knight, Miranda Arnold, Megan Cooke, Kelly Markham, and Bianca Smith: I would be lost without you. Please never leave me.

To AS Teague, my wife, I mean, not actually my wife, but we have slept in a lot of beds together and on more than one occasion I was drunk and naked. But that's an awkward story for another day. I have no words. My life would be a mess without you. Literally and figuratively. HA! Thank you for always being there to listen to me bitch and for plotting out what I'm writing for the day each and every morning. Everyone needs an Ashley. They just can't have mine.

To JJL: I can honestly say I would not be where I am today without these ladies. Every day we talk. Every day we laugh. Every day they teach me something new. And every day, I go to their houses, stare through their windows, and plot how I'm going to kidnap them and keep them locked away in my basement forever. Okay, so maybe one of those things isn't true. But I'll let you decide which one. Sidenote: I have a lot of frequent flyer miles saved up from when Meghan was in Belize.

To Mo: My Mo. The laziest bottom in the world who disappoints me on a daily basis, because, in reality, she isn't lazy at all. She's brilliant and funny. She's supportive and loyal. She can give a mean shoulder kiss and then turn around and write the hottest hand-job you have ever read. That's my girl!

To: Lana Kart: My hooker. Thank you for making me gorgeous teasers! And really, just for being an all-around amazing whore. (Is that enough insults?)

To Tina Snider: Thank you for all your help with the Winery and for helping beta The Darkest Sunrise. You rock!

To Jessica Estep: You came in on this one with guns blazing. I've been doing this since 2014, and I don't know how I ever released a book without you. Thank you for being amazing.

To Alissa Smith: Thank you for putting up with me. HAHA! I don't know how many times I've messaged you asking for something to be done immediately and never once have you told me you can't. You always get it done. You are an incredible woman and mother. Your boys are lucky to have you.

To Mickey Reed: Please don't read these acknowledgments…. they haven't been edited. HAHA! Thank you for making this book great!

To Julie Deaton: The Ultimate Proofreader. You are a rockstar. And because of this, you are stuck with me forever. No take backs!

To Stacey Blake: This woman…I swear. If there is ever a problem with my book, she will fix it…like twenty-two seconds after I email her. Regardless that it's 3 a.m. on Sunday night. Okay, maybe that's a bit of a stretch…but not a long one.

To Jay Aheer: I can't say enough about this woman's cover designs. She gave me something unique and gorgeous when this story turned a little darker than I expected.

To Hang Le: Thank you for not killing me. HAHAHA!

To Wander Aguiar: Thank you for capturing the perfect pictures for Porter and Charlotte. And when we struggled, Andrey jumped right in, spending hours scouring through hundreds of images until we found them. Bravo, gentlemen.

To Staci Hart, Ilsa Madden-Mills, and Brittainy Cherry: I want to thank you for the amazing advice y'all gave me when I was developing this release plan. And then I promptly want to follow that up with an apology for all of the "HALP ME!" messages y'all received shortly after. HA! You ladies are the absolute best!

And last, but very not least, to the man who has made this dream a reality. Mike, 2016 was a crazy year for us. But through it all…I love you. Even when I hated you. So pretty much, like, every day. Thank you for loving me. Thank you for supporting me. And most of all… Thank you for this crazy and beautiful life.

OTHER BOOKS

THE DARKEST SUNRISE DUET
The Darkest Sunrise
The Brightest Sunset

THE RETRIEVAL DUET
Retrieval
Transfer

The Fall Up
The Spiral Down

THE WRECKED AND RUINED SERIES
Changing Course
Stolen Course
Broken Course
Among the Echoes

ON THE ROPES
Fighting Silence
Fighting Shadows
Fighting Solutude

GUARDIAN PROTECTION SERIES
Singe

ABOUT THE AUTHOR

Born and raised in Savannah, Georgia, Aly Martinez is a stay-at-home mom to four crazy kids under the age of five, including a set of twins. Currently living in South Carolina, she passes what little free time she has reading anything and everything she can get her hands on, preferably with a glass of wine at her side.

After some encouragement from her friends, Aly decided to add "Author" to her ever-growing list of job titles. So grab a glass of Chardonnay, or a bottle if you're hanging out with Aly, and join her aboard the crazy train she calls life.

Facebook: www.facebook.com/AuthorAlyMartinez

Twitter: twitter.com/AlyMartinezAuth

Goodreads: www.goodreads.com/AlyMartinez

Made in the USA
Lexington, KY
15 June 2018